Carolina Dream

Southern Breeze Series, Book 1

Regina Rudd Merrick

Scrivenings
PRESS
Quench your thirst for story.
www.ScriveningsPress.com

©2020 Regina Merrick

Published by Scrivenings Press LLC
15 Lucky Lane
Morrilton, Arkansas 72110
https://ScriveningsPress.com

Printed in the United States of America

Paperback ISBN 978-1-64917-072-9

eBook ISBN 978-1-64917-073-6

Library of Congress Control Number: 2020940055

Cover by Diane Turpin, www.dianeturpindesigns.com

(Note: This book was previously published by Mantle Rock Publishing LLC and was re-published when MRP was acquired by Scrivenings Press LLC in 2020.)

DEDICATION

To Granny, Dorothy Imogene Brown Rudd (1920-2013), who gave me the gifts of music and romance novels. She gave me her piano and shared her Grace Livingston Hill novels with me, both of which have made me the person I am today.

ACKNOWLEDGMENTS

There are so many people to thank when considering this endeavor called book-writing.

First, and foremost, I thank my God for giving me not only the desire, but the strength and imagination to complete that first manuscript. He is my Lord and Savior, and the Desire of my heart.

To my husband, Todd Merrick, thank you for being the love of my life and my encouragement in all things. Your support and confidence in me has been overwhelming. Thank you for believing in me.

Emily Merrick and Ellen Merrick, my two grown-up baby girls, thank you for not thinking I'm weird for putting myself out there with something as intimate as my thoughts on the written page. You are amazing young women.

To my extended family – parents, Richard and Wanda Rudd; in-laws, James and Margaret Merrick; sisters and brothers - thank you for your spiritual guidance, unconditional love, and confidence that I can create not only music, but literature, from my heart. You've blessed me with your excitement about every phase of this venture.

To my friend, Pam Collins, thank you for listening to me, for getting me out of my comfort zone, and for encouraging me to listen to that niggling voice inside of me that said, "do it!" Lucy is definitely patterned after you.

To my church family at Marion Baptist, thank you for being my safe haven, my outlet for the musician in me, and my second family. I can't wait to spend eternity with you!

Posthumous thanks to novelists Grace Livingston Hill, Emilie Loring, Laura Ingalls Wilder, and Essie Summers, all deceased, but all living through their writing. They all influenced me greatly, and wrote Christian Fiction before Christian Fiction was cool.

To the ladies of the Inkspirational Messages blog, and the former "RomanceFanfiction.net" site, thank you for reading, for encouraging, for being a sounding board for ideas.

To all my Crittenden County Public Library people, if it weren't for being around all of you and all of those books, I would never think I could write one. Bob Yehling, thank you for offering writing classes in our library, and encouraging me during this season I thought would never really happen.

To the members of the KenTen Writers Group, thank you for showing me that I do have a writing voice, and helping me to grow as a writer.

To editor and friend Pam Harris, thank you for being honest in your edits and faithful in your encouragement.

And lastly, thanks to Mantle Rock Publishing, Jerry and Kathy Cretsinger, for having faith in my book, and in me, even after taking out their flag pole with my car upon our first meeting.

Delight yourself also in the Lord, and He shall give you the desires of your heart.

Psalm 37:4 NKJV

CHAPTER ONE

March

The house was quiet. The crowd that had milled around the main floor of the mansion finally dissipated around five o'clock that afternoon, and Jared Benton was finally alone. He took in the polished mahogany sideboard and table, the formal velvet drapes, the gleaming hardwood floors. It wasn't the same without Alex. It had been a haven—a place where he knew acceptance and generosity.

Now? Now it was just a big house full of memories, and would be passed along to the next owner. He took off the well-tailored suit jacket and laid it across a dining chair, then pulled at his tie. It felt like a noose around his neck after an interminable day.

His attention was caught by a soft sniffle.

"Bright Eyes?"

Jared looked up to see Prudie, still in her black funeral dress, just inside the dining room archway of Alex Crawford's 1859 mansion. He stood there a minute, his half-smile aimed at the old woman. He saw that her handkerchief was still in her hand, where he'd seen it earlier. She dabbed at her nose and eyes as she tried to erase evidence of that sniffle. He laid the letter back on the table and walked over to her. "Prudie, I thought I told you to go on home."

"I couldn't leave until I'd seen you again." She turned her face to him with a watery smile and put her hand on his arm. "Amazing how time flies, isn't it? It seems like just yesterday that I saw a skinny teenager poke his head in the back door looking for a glass of water on a hot summer day. Now you're a man grown." She patted his arm and swiped a tear from her eye. Her head shook with frustration.

Usually a tough old bird, her employer's death had hit her harder than even she expected. Jared watched as she tried her best to get the stiffening back in her spine as if she needed to set a good example for him. "But enough of that. I wanted to let you know I left some apple pie on the kitchen table if you want to take some home with you."

He hugged the elderly housekeeper, thankful to have someone to mourn with. "Thanks, Prudie. You make the best, you know."

"Well, that's what Mr. Alex used to say. My, but I'm going to miss that old codger." She blew her nose loudly as she shook her head.

"Yeah. Me, too. You go on home and get some rest, you hear?"

"I will." She stretched up to kiss him on the cheek, and started to turn toward the doorway when she noticed what was in his hand. "I see you got that letter."

"You knew about it?"

"He tried a few things out on me before he wrote the final draft." Her eyes sparkled as she grinned at him. She looked him straight in the eye. A tear threatened to escape before she dabbed it with the hankie. "You were the light of his life, you know that?"

"Thanks, Prudie." He looked down. He didn't want to look into her face just now. He was hesitant to let go of the emotions that still washed over him at the thought of his friend and mentor being gone forever.

He glanced up at her, finally, as she stood there silently. She looked as if she wanted to say something, but she didn't. "I'll go on now. Call me if you need me, okay?" When he nodded, she gave a little snort of humor and shook her head wearily. "I'm so tired right now I think if I go home and sit in a rocker, I may never get up."

He grinned at her, trying to imagine the bundle of seventy-year-old energy giving in to a life of retirement. He couldn't see it. "I have a feeling there will be some changes around here."

She gave him a keen look. "I know. Just remember, all change ain't bad."

"I'll try to keep that in mind." He felt a coldness creep into his heart as he thought of what he had learned that day.

She shook her head at the grim expression on his face as he turned back to the table and took the letter in his hand, only to shove it into the top drawer of the sideboard.

April

SARAH JANE CRAWFORD whipped her little Ford sedan into the parking lot in front of the small Kentucky high school and fluffed her long brown hair with her fingers. Brown, but with reddish highlights, it had just enough curl to give her the option of going curly on a rushed day or straightening it out when she had time. Today was a curly day.

She adjusted the rearview mirror. Hair and makeup. Check. Her smile widened, and she looked at herself carefully. No food in her teeth. Check. She bobbed her head at the hazel-eyed girl in the mirror, took a deep breath, and prepared herself to face a day filled with hormonal teenagers.

Late again, she hurried in the front door. The dream that she had been enjoying before the alarm woke her from a peaceful slumber clouded her thoughts. She signed in at the school office and picked up her mail. She simply couldn't get away from the disconnected images of a huge mansion, the smell of sea and marsh, and deep brown eyes. Shaking her head to clear it, she made her way to the office adjacent to the music room. It was a dream. A silly dream. Why couldn't she forget it? Spring fever. Had to be.

Shoving the thought aside, she grimaced at the rickety 1970s-era olive-green cart that held all the textbooks and materials that she used to teach music. The newest teacher in the school, she didn't have her own classroom, but instead dealt with a different room in a different part of the building every period except the last. At least during seventh period she had dibs on the one and only music room – the band room – for her favorite class of the day: high school chorus.

In a daze, Sarah pushed the cart down the hall toward classroom 101. She would have walked right past it; the only thing getting her attention was the jolt that came when she pushed the cart over an uneven spot in the floor. She caught the cymbals and small snare drum before they tumbled to the floor. Talk about starting off the day with a bang.

Sarah's best friend, Lucy, came from just inside the door of her own domain, classroom 103.

"I thought that sounded like you. Sarah, wait up." The petite blonde bounced toward Sarah and followed her into her classroom. She picked a stray hair off Sarah's back when she turned. "I thought you'd never get here. Listen, are you busy tonight?"

A special education teacher, the five-foot-two-inch dynamo had perfected the art of the fix-up. She had fixed Sarah up with nearly every single male teacher in the district or outlying areas, various young men from church, the new mailman, or any likely contender.

"No. What did you have in mind?" Sarah narrowed her eyes.

She hoped it wasn't another blind date – although, in a town this small, blind dates were rather more likely to be "slightly nearsighted" dates. Lucy had tried for weeks to talk her into getting out more.

"I thought maybe a girls' night out would be fun for a change." Lucy green eyes sparkled when she smiled.

"What other kinds of nights out do we ever have? They're mostly 'girls' nights out,' if you haven't noticed!" Sarah laughed.

Lucy giggled, her mouth twisting in a pert grin. "You're right, but I mean the kind that includes a spa treatment: massage, facial, pedicure, the works. I found a spa that has evening hours for times like this . . ." Lucy stopped short when she saw Sarah's expression. Her voice flattened as she put her hands on her hips and arched her brow. "I know what you're thinking."

"Oh, do you?" Sensing a plot against her, Sarah sent her a mock glare.

"Yes, I can see those wheels turning. Your first thought was 'and just what time is it?' Okay, you asked, I'll answer."

Sarah simply raised her eyebrows.

Lucy would not be daunted. "It's no time in particular . . . but it is spring . . ."

"Uh . . . yes. April in Kentucky is about as 'spring' as you can get—although those snow flurries last week made me wish someone had talked me into a trip to somewhere, anywhere warmer than Chicago for spring break."

Lucy rolled her eyes and continued her argument. "You'll never let me live that down, will you? But we had fun, didn't we? Besides, we could never have afforded the hotel and those theatre tickets in June, now could we? Anyway, it's spring, prom is next weekend, and since we're both chaperones—well, it wouldn't hurt us any to set a good example for our students." She shrugged her shoulders and tilted her head in all seriousness.

Sarah caught the gleam in her eyes. If Lucy spent half the time working on securing a relationship for herself as she did for Sarah, she would probably be married with two kids by now. She had hoped that Lucy wouldn't push her toward the assistant football coach again. He was a nice guy, good-looking in a big, outdoorsy sort of way, and they had gone out a couple of times. But the spark Sarah dreamed about—just this morning in fact—simply wasn't there.

She had felt that spark once. At least she thought she had.

Sarah looked away and tried to wipe away the frown gathering between her dark brows. Not a frown of anger, but of disappointment. She shook her head and looked at her friend. Cocking her head to one side, she took in a deep breath. "Lucy, I would be happy to go to the spa with you, but not with the end product in mind of luring a certain football coach. Let's just go and have some fun. No guys and no strings attached. Please?" Sarah gave Lucy a pleading look. Don't bring up past ghosts. Not now, anyway.

Lucy nodded in sympathy and glanced toward the door. Students were arriving in the hallway. She lowered her voice, and her demeanor grew serious. "Are you all right?"

Sarah nodded and glanced up at the clock to see that it was almost time for class to start. "I'd better get going."

Lucy shot a keen glance at her friend. "Something's happened, hasn't it?"

When Sarah avoided her glance, Lucy sighed and nodded. "Okay, I'll let it go. For now. No strings attached – just a simple girls' night out." Before she turned to go back to her own classroom, she quirked an eyebrow and gave Sarah a triumphant grin. "Oh . . . and by the way, I have us appointments for six p.m. tonight. See ya."

Lucy fluttered her fingers in a wave and flew toward her classroom. Sarah shook her head. The "unsinkable Molly Brown" had nothing on Lucy Dixon.

SHOWERED and ready for an evening at the spa with Lucy, Sarah paused at her kitchen table to go through some forgotten mail that she had absent-mindedly pitched there when she brought it in from the box the day before. The whistled tune coming from her lips matched the slight smile on her face.

She shuffled through the random items, and two pieces caught her eye. The first was a smaller, square envelope. She looked at the postmark, then at the back to see if there was a return address. When she saw the name, she stared at it for a moment, then put it down. Staring into space, she sank into a chair and sat there a moment before she gathered her wits about her. It wasn't like she didn't know it was coming. She'd heard, after all, that they had become engaged, and she even knew the date and time of the wedding without the aid of an invitation.

There were people in the community, close-knit though it might be, that simply couldn't wait to let little tidbits of information like that drop, just to see what her reaction would be. She didn't give them the satisfaction of wearing her heart on her sleeve, and she wasn't going to think about it right now.

She couldn't.

If she did, she would be a mess, and the last thing she wanted was to go into it with Lucy tonight. Eventually, she'd talk about it. But not now. She squeezed her eyes shut, and her hand on her chest pressed in, trying to ease the ache that wanted so desperately to come out, preferably in waves of tears. Surely,

surely she didn't have any tears left for this, did she? Wasn't she the one who had undoubtedly been saved from a life of heartbreak and uncertainty?

Enough. This was not going to ruin her weekend. She picked up the other envelope, a business-sized letter, and frowned at the postmark. South Carolina? Her eyebrows scrunched as she studied the envelope, and true to habit and genetics, her lips pursed thoughtfully. She caught a glimpse of herself in the door of the microwave. She was turning into her mother, and in turn, her grandmother.

The return address wasn't familiar and indicated a law firm. The fine-linen envelope felt luxurious. She reached into the drawer for a knife and carefully slit the envelope open, removing the letter printed on heavy stationery. Probably junk mail, one of those free trips for placing a magazine subscription order.

Tossing the envelope on the counter, she read the letter:

To: Mr. Robert Crawford, Mrs. Susan Crawford Harris, Ms. Sarah J. Crawford

From: Bodine, Schumaker, and Lentz, Attorneys At Law

RE: Alexander Rudd Crawford estate

MR. CRAWFORD, *Mrs. Harris, and Ms. Crawford,*

OUR FIRM WAS GIVEN *the task to locate the relatives of Mr. Alexander Rudd Crawford of Litchfield Beach, South Carolina. We regret to inform you that while Mr. Crawford's wish was to meet you before his death, illness precluded this. Even so, it was his desire that his good fortune be passed on to blood relatives; therefore, you were named beneficiaries of a portion of Mr. Crawford's estate.*

. . .

Please contact us as soon as possible to make arrangements concerning this inheritance. We look forward to hearing from you.

Sincerely,

Mr. Thomas William Schumaker, *Attorney At Law*
Charleston, SC

Alexander Crawford? The name sounded familiar . . . Sarah glanced at the phone. Did Dad get one of these letters? Maybe he would know what this was about.

About to pick up the phone to call her dad, it rang. She checked the Caller-ID and glanced down at the unopened square envelope. Glad that she didn't have to open it now, she answered the phone, pressing "talk" on the second ring.

"Hi, Dad. Do you know what's going on?"

"Okay, so you're telling me that you got this letter from an attorney in North Carolina."

"South Carolina, Luce."

"Right. South Carolina. And there's some kind of inheritance, but you don't know what it is, or who it's from."

"Well, actually, we have heard of Alexander Crawford. But we've never met him."

The spa experience had been all that they hoped for. They were pampered, plucked, and preened to the point of sedation, but after a massage that left them both almost giddy, they decided that pasta was in order to finish the evening.

Maybe it was the massage, or maybe it was just that the

information was about to burst out of her if she didn't tell someone, but she couldn't keep her newfound knowledge from Lucy one more second. She never had kept things from Lucy— well, except for the dream.

"So you have a rich uncle that you didn't know was rich and he had no heirs so they found you guys? How cool is that?" Lucy had been shaking her head in disbelief for a half-hour.

Sarah laughed. "I know, right? And I thought this would be an awful day when I got up this morning." She looked down at the plate of cooling pasta and speared a forkful of noodles. When she looked up, Lucy was gazing at her intently, much like earlier that morning.

"What else has happened?" Her eyes were narrowed, also much like this morning. "I can tell, and you don't go around talking about days being awful unless it means something. You are little Mary Sunshine, usually. But I can tell. Give."

Sarah glanced up at the waiter who came to check on them. "Could we get dipping sauce for the breadsticks?" When the waiter walked away, Sarah heaved a deep sigh. "I got an invitation in the mail yesterday."

"Marc?"

"A wedding invitation. I still haven't opened it." Sarah nodded and pressed the cloth napkin to her lips for a second. "But you know, it's okay. I didn't even cry this time."

"Maybe you should." Lucy shook her head and rolled her eyes in obvious frustration. "Honestly, Sarah."

Sarah's eyes grew round. "No. Don't you see? God's given me a chance. What if I'd married him and then found out about Alice?" She was trying to convince Lucy as much as herself.

Lucy paused and twisted her lips in disgust. "I met her at a meeting a few weeks ago."

"You didn't tell me." Sarah looked up in surprise.

Lucy shrugged. "No big deal. It was at one of those regional meetings, and some of the other counties sent their teachers.

She seems nice." Her arched eyebrow told Sarah how irritating that thought was for her.

"I'm sure she is." Sarah's shoulders drooped. "Do you think it was me?"

"Don't backtrack now, Sarah. And no, it wasn't you. And really, I don't think it was even Marc."

"God's providence?"

"You're the one that said it, not me." Lucy arched an eyebrow and stretched herself as tall as her petite frame would allow, then clamped her lips together in a thin line. Sarah began to feel the love that God had given her through this crazy girl. "Enough about two-timing boyfriends. You've got bigger fish to fry, my friend."

Sarah felt excitement surge through her. Lucy was right. Enough is enough. The mystery of the inheritance took over her thoughts once again. "You're right. Who has time for such folderol as marriage, anyway? We heiresses must attend to the business at hand."

Lucy picked up a fresh breadstick, broke it in two, and then handed half to Sarah. They both dipped the broken end into the rich, creamy Alfredo sauce. "A toast. To Sarah and the Crawford fortune." They tapped their breadsticks together and giggled noisily, causing other dinner guests to smile at the two young women biting into what they knew heaven must taste like.

CHAPTER TWO

*S*arah looked at the clock when she woke up, then groaned. Nine-thirty. Her mother would say she had slept her Saturday away.

She slowly came to herself, and the events of the previous day came into focus. The Crawford and Harris families of Summerville, Kentucky, were beneficiaries of an unknown relative's estate. The call to Mr. Schumaker didn't reveal much except that someone in the family would be required to appear in South Carolina to assume responsibility for the estate. No idea of the extent of the estate, just that there was property involved. When Sarah told her dad about it, he laughed and said it was probably mortgaged to the hilt.

The spa treatment and night out had been just what she needed to get her mind off things. For once, she was so relaxed by the time she went to bed that she didn't have the dream. Why did she feel so silly about a dream? She still hadn't told Lucy about it, for some reason. They had been so busy talking about this and that, and then she broke down and told her about the inheritance.

She lay there in the shaft of sun that had eased its way

through the crack between her curtains and stretched the kinks of a hard week out of her tired body. She stared at the ceiling and tried with all her might to recall more of the dream that she had seen, bit by bit, in her mind's eye, more times than she cared to admit. It had to mean something.

Random images floated through her mind. There was a house—she knew that much. There was a man with brown eyes —a very handsome man, if memory served. Sometimes God spoke through dreams, didn't he? Look at Joseph. He probably wasn't very happy with his situation, just like her. Well, maybe their situations weren't all that similar—she hadn't been sold into slavery and thrown into prison. But Joseph would probably understand why she felt unsure of her next step. Her dad, and probably Joseph as well, would tell her that's where faith comes in. But the timing of that letter from the lawyer—something about it made her feel tingly all over.

Oliver sat on the floor at her bedside, his tail thumping, and he began to wriggle happily when he saw that she was awake. When he worked his nose up and under her hand, she turned her head toward him and smirked. "I'm up, buddy." Sarah threw back the quilt that she kept on her bed year-round. The weight of the cover always comforted her. It almost enticed her to turn over and go back to sleep, but there was just something not quite right about her lack of activity when there had been so much daylight spent already.

She pulled on the shorts and t-shirt she'd worn after school the day before. It looked as if today would be as warm as yesterday. On her way through the kitchen she hit the button on the coffee maker to start her Saturday morning ritual. She hurried to the door to let Oliver out and then automatically filled his food dish next to the back door of the kitchen. Bright sunlight filtered through the window above the kitchen sink as she relaxed there, waiting for her first cup of java of the day. It would be a nice morning to go for a run, but she was too relaxed. She didn't want to undo the pampering she had received the night before. She rotated her shoulders and neck, enjoying the looseness of the muscles that had been coaxed to relaxation. When she saw Oliver roll in the early spring green grass, she sighed happily. Maybe tonight.

The mail that she had looked at before she talked to her dad and then left with Lucy still rested on the counter: the letter from the lawyer open where she had read it, the square, formal envelope still sealed shut.

The aroma coming from the coffee maker drew her back to the pot, so she waited for the freshly-brewed coffee to finish and Oliver to bark at the back door. She turned her eyes to that one piece of mail that she had accidentally-on-purpose abandoned. Picking it up, a familiar ache spread inside her chest. It had to be an invitation to his wedding. The back of the envelope was sealed with a monogram. The fancy calligraphy showed a large "M" in the center, flanked by an "m" and an "a" in smaller, silver filigree script. She took a deep breath and decided to get it over with, then simply opened the envelope. Her suspicions were confirmed.

June 12. That was the date she had heard. No turning back now. She might be over Marc, and last night she might have talked herself out of being depressed over his defection, but in the cold light of day, it still hurt. And it not only hurt, but it also made her angry.

She knew, without a doubt, that she wanted to be conveniently out of town when it came time for the wedding. It could be Timbuktu or the North Pole for all she cared. She just wanted to be anywhere but Summerville.

Still holding the invitation between two fingers, she shook her head furiously as her heart rate increased. All the sense and good will she espoused the night before turned to dust. She wanted to slam something, throw something, break something, scream. But there was a better way. A more permanent way.

15

She reached into the drawer next to the sink and pulled out the butane lighter she used for the grill and kept handy for lighting candles. She tore the invitation in pieces and placed them in the sink. After pulling the trigger of the lighter, she held it to the ripped edges. Her breathing eased as the acrid scent of burning paper reached her nostrils and the fancy script turned black and then shattered as it burned up.

After she rinsed the residue out of the basin and opened the window above the sink to dispel the smoke, she inhaled deeply, pursed her lips, and nodded. Decision made. She felt better. She was about to start a new phase of her life.

She picked up the phone and punched in her parents' number. "Dad, I think I may just take you up on that offer to head to South Carolina ahead of you guys."

June

JARED BENTON once again stood looking out the window of the formal dining room at Pilot Oaks. The trees were in full leaf, and the azaleas were well past their blooming season. The clumps of Palmetto trees, always green, always a symbol of the warm South Carolina climate, waved in the hot sunshine. Alex had died in the warmth of springtime, and now it was almost summer.

He leaned his hand against the window frame and allowed his shoulders to slump. Finally. He had held it together for months now. Alex Crawford -- his mentor, his ally, his friend, his business partner -- was dead, and strangers traveled even now to claim their inheritance. Common supposition had thought Jared would inherit everything. Common supposition had been wrong.

He turned from the window and looked at Will Schumaker, his friend and his lawyer. "I guess they're on their way. "

"I talked to Robert Crawford yesterday, and everything is on schedule for his daughter, Sarah." Will looked down at the notepad on the table. "Arrival on June 11, meeting on June 16. Give her a few days to relax and enjoy the area, and then we meet middle of next week. Did you leave her condo key and packet in the box?"

Jared lifted an eyebrow at his question. He'd do his job, but don't ask for a welcoming committee. "You know I did. Does she even know the real estate business is part of the inheritance?"

Will shrugged. "No. They weren't to know anything about the extent of the inheritance until they come down to claim it. I guess he thought that way they wouldn't take the money and run."

Jared's face twisted in a nervous frown. "And you know they're legit?"

A loud sigh emanated before Will answered him. "Jared . . . they didn't come looking for Alex. He went looking for them, and they didn't even know it."

He weighed his words while he looked down at the well-polished toes of his black dress shoes. When he looked up, lips pursed in determination, he had made a decision. "I'll buy them out, Will. I have to."

"It may not be your decision. The will states that the Crawford family in Kentucky will inherit sixty percent of the business and the entire house." Will got up from the table and walked over to Jared. He put his hand on the younger man's shoulder. "You know the will wasn't all about the inheritance. Alex talked to me a lot those last few months he was so sick. He talked to me about you, too. Your future was important to him. He didn't want you tied down to the point you didn't have a life outside of the business."

Jared twisted his lips and stared out the window. A gliding gull drew his attention to the summerhouse. His chest tightened at the memory of Alex and the conversations they had held in that summerhouse. They talked about life, about the future, and about what Jared wanted out of life. The old structure had come to be a haven of sorts, a place for prayer and reflection, and now it might be out of reach.

"He was pretty important to me, too." Jared cleared his throat of the lump that threatened to choke him. When he looked up, Will held out an envelope toward him.

"Prudie found it when she oversaw the cleaning after the funeral."

He shook his head and looked at the lawyer. "I know. I should have read it before now. What did the old goat have to say that wasn't for public consumption?"

Will shrugged as he handed him the sealed envelope. "See for yourself."

Jared reached out and took the letter. Alex's angular writing made him miss the old man even more.

"I'll see myself out. Call me if you have any questions."

"Will do." Jared looked down at the letter, then back at Will. "Thanks."

A raised hand and half-smile answered as Will left the room.

He looked down at the envelope, then tapped it against his left hand as he went through the central foyer to the library and a comfortable chair. Best to get this over with.

Dear Jared,

I never was fortunate enough to call a young man "son," but when I think about you, it's the first word that comes to my mind. I know you're probably aggravated at me about this new will I had drawn up. Don't blame you. But it's mine to give, so I expect you to behave like the professional you are and make sure my relatives know as much about the business as you can teach them so they can make an informed decision.

You know my story. I never knew my parents or brothers. My Dorothy was taken away from me before we knew the joy of raising a family of our own, and because of that, I tried my best to turn off the part of me that could love. I missed out. I know that now. I spent my time and energy building a business that couldn't love me back. When it dawned on me God wasn't finished with me, it was too late to find a partner for life.

So rather than find me a wife, I found me a grandson. You. I know you're hurting, son, but don't let it run your life. There's a lot of life still left to live, and I intend you to find the one God has for you. She won't care what happened before, because God's been getting her ready all along. Maybe she's hurt, too.

I don't pretend to predict the future. I know I want you to keep an open mind. Don't let Annabelle haunt you, boy.

Stay strong, and when you don't know what to do, just do the next right thing.

Alex

The sun slanted in the windows, on its way down, when Jared folded the letter and slid it back in the envelope. He would read it again when just thinking about Alex didn't still make him notice the lead weight in the pit of his stomach, even after three months. Later, but not now.

He shook his head, one side of his mouth twisted upward in a reluctant grin at the very thought of the man who had written the letter. He would admit, he wasn't really happy with the situation, but he had no choice but to accept it.

Accept it, and do the next right thing.

CHAPTER THREE

June

Sarah had until the end of the month to decide whether to return to her teaching position in August, but right now her biggest decision was whether to choose the drive-through at McDonald's or Arby's on her solitary road trip to Litchfield Beach, South Carolina. Well, not too solitary – Oliver was with her. Who needs a man when you have a great big hunk of dog? Her mom hadn't been too crazy about the idea of a solo trip, but her dad reminded her that Sarah was a big girl now.

She wouldn't even think about school until after she met the lawyer from the letter. She had a whole month to settle the estate of this unknown relative before her contract deadline, and then she could make that decision. Lucy was the only one who knew the real reason she had decided to head out to South Carolina early. Her parents and sister wouldn't be able to come down until the next week, if needed, but she had to get out of town. There was a wedding she had to avoid at all costs. She would tell them later, but for now, she just wanted to get the heck out of Dodge.

The letter from the South Carolina law firm came at an opportune time. Even before it arrived, she was restless, just a little out of sorts in a lot of ways. It was as if a wave of quiet dissatisfaction had come upon her, and nothing she did to change things in her life seemed to make it go away. Prayer, Bible study . . . God had been suspiciously quiet.

When it seemed that the school year would never end, she had prayed for something to happen . . . for anything to happen. And it did, in the form of a letter from a law firm in South Carolina. She was grateful when she thought about the tears and the prayers that had been sent heavenward and realized, not for the first time, that God always came through.

Maybe I just needed a vacation, she thought halfway through the long drive through Kentucky, Tennessee, North Carolina, and then finally to South Carolina. As she had taken in the grandeur of the Great Smoky Mountains of Tennessee, she had felt a flurry of excitement that she hadn't experienced in a long time.

"All right, God, you've got me all to yourself for the next few weeks. I expect some real communication about what to do with myself. I know I haven't exactly been a fan of change in the past, but at this point I'm ready for whatever it is that you have in store."

NOT LONG BEFORE HE DIED, Alex had shown Jared all the information he had gleaned about the Crawford family in Kentucky. He had photocopies of high school and college yearbook pictures, college transcripts, wedding and birth announcements – all of which he gave to Jared. He wanted him to know this family he intended to be a part of his life, even if it occurred after his death.

What was he supposed to do with this knowledge? It didn't

seem quite fair, somehow, that he knew about them, but they didn't have a clue he even existed.

And now, she was here. Here and unarmed.

It had kept him awake and in prayer several nights since Alex passed in March. And now Alex's letter had given him even more to think about—a lot to pray about, too.

Jared sat at the small bistro table on his deck overlooking the beach, soaking in the strengthening rays of the rising sun. He was not a morning person, but when he woke up at five a.m., he figured he may as well get up, and if nothing else, pray.

Jared snorted and shook his head. If nothing else. "I know, God, you think I'm pretty arrogant, don't you?"

Sarah Jane Crawford was here, minutes away, and she had no idea Jared Benton existed, much less that he was praying for her family.

And he was. It had occurred to him that God had a plan, for not only himself, but also this family that had inadvertently been sucked into the same vortex he had been swirling in for months.

He wanted to see her, maybe get an edge on her. That's all. A good businessman looked at all the angles, right? Her picture made her look like a pleasant person, but then how much do you really know from a college yearbook? She was a musician. A teacher. So what would she know about real estate? There was that nagging voice inside his head again. He knew exactly where it was coming from. It was the same voice of doubt that plagued him off and on the last ten years. It was the "it's too good to be true" voice that told him not to trust.

He didn't want to meet her before Wednesday, but he wanted to watch her. See her interact with other people. His eyebrows shifted down. It sounded creepy, even to him.

But not creepy enough to keep him away from North Litchfield Beach, which was where he had a feeling she would head as soon as she finished her breakfast. In ten minutes, he had put on his swim trunks, jumped in his convertible Jaguar XJ, and made his way to the Sandpiper Condominium complex.

SARAH ARRIVED in Litchfield Beach a few days ahead of her appointment with the lawyer. This was her vacation, and she planned to treat it as such. Even though she was alone, she was looking forward to every opportunity to sit on the beach and read as well as go for walks or run along the water's edge. If she wanted to get out, she would drive around and take in the sights or shop at the outlet malls up the road at Myrtle Beach. When she sat on the balcony of the condo the first evening, the sea oats and sea grasses waving gracefully at her from the dunes that separated the beach from the high-rise relaxed her like nothing else ever had.

A few years earlier she, her sister and brother-in-law, and her parents had come to Litchfield Beach, a place unknown to them but recommended by a friend, to celebrate their parents' wedding anniversary. They all agreed that it was the best family vacation ever. There was a connection there that she never could seem to shake. Her family teased her about her "South Carolina frame of mind."

Today was Saturday, the day Marc was getting married. Not to her. But it was okay. She was okay. God was good, and He had brought her here at the right time.

Waking in the king-sized bed to the sound of the surf hitting the beach and the sun coming up over the water through the crack between the closed drapes made her happy. Content, even. At least for now. She had never told anyone, but she had always dreamed of living close to the water. Why, she didn't know. She'd grown up landlocked except for lakes and rivers, but there was something about the ocean that drew her, gave her peace.

She made coffee and ate her cheese Danish. The water beckoned. As she and Oliver walked along the veranda toward the boardwalk, she noticed there were only a few people on the beach.

"You know, Ollie, maybe there are perks involved in having the same name as the real estate company. Who knows?" Her happy grin spilled over into a laugh as Oliver began to drag her down the walkway. Just about the time they reached the top of the wooden stairs leading down to the beach, they came to a halt.

AFTER AN HOUR ON THE BEACH, he gave up. She wasn't coming. Of course, it was only eight o'clock. Maybe she wasn't an early riser either. Heat rippled up from the sand. The sand crabs scrambled for shade as they burrowed in the sand. It always amazed him. But they had the right idea. He couldn't dig into the sand, but he could jump in the ocean and cool off.

After his swim, he jogged down the beach and dried off enough to get into his car. He made his way to the steps of the boardwalk that traversed the dunes between beach and civilization. As he reached the top, a flurry of brindle fur and a happy tongue almost caught him unaware. He righted himself before he fell backward.

"Whoa! Slow down, there, buddy!" He laughed at the friendly pooch and looked up at his owner.

It was her.

And he couldn't stop staring.

A flawless complexion, blue eyes—or were they green? Long hair pulled up on top of her head with a clip. A modest suit tantalized enough to make him know she was an attractive young lady. Attractive? More like beautiful. And she was, on some level, according to that nagging voice inside, the enemy.

Sarah's face reddened as she pulled at the leash. "Oliver! I don't know what's wrong with him. Usually he's suspicious of strange men, but he acts like he's just found his best friend. Please excuse him."

Jared found his voice. He swallowed thickly and smiled. "No apologies necessary. I'm a dog-lover myself, but I don't have one right now. Always did as a kid, though."

Sarah grinned. "You seem to know dogs. You found his favorite spot to be rubbed."

Jared rubbed Oliver's ears and chest vigorously, going for the spots that reduced the pup to a quivering mass of happiness. She was watching him curiously. Maybe her eyes were gray?

"You staying here at the Sandpiper?" He stood and stepped to one side to give her room to pass.

"Yes, we got here last night. And you?"

"No, I work around here. Just checking things out." He avoided her eyes. He didn't like lying to her. And he wasn't. He *was* checking things out. Mainly her.

"Seems nice."

"It is. Listen, have a great stay, and don't forget the sunscreen. Watch out for this guy. He seems to make friends easily." He held his hand up and took his leave, while Sarah and Oliver made their way down the steps and into the sand.

SARAH TOOK her flip-flops off at the bottom the steps, wiggling her toes in the warm sand. Before they went down the steps, she had looked back as he walked the length of the boardwalk. His hair was oh, so dark, and his eyes? His eyes were like dark chocolate—her favorite kind.

She looked down at her partner for the day. "I wonder if all the handymen around here are that good-looking. Or maybe he's the pool-boy."

She gathered up her bag and giggled as Oliver pulled on the leash, and then headed down to the area just before the line where the surf had hardened the wet sand down to a perfect running surface. Letting the retractable leash out a good ten feet, Sarah looped the leash around her hand and walked into the gentle surf. She dug her toes into the sand, closed her eyes for a moment, and then opened them, reveling in the vastness of the Atlantic Ocean. She would go in for a swim later, but now she began to stretch, warming up for a good run after a day in the car. Oliver began to move closer to the rippling waves, but he came back and sat patiently, his head cocked at his mistress.

"You're a silly boy, Oliver. Did you think you knew him?" If only. Her smile widened. If she were to pick out a model for the man in her dream, this man on the boardwalk, tan and fit, wearing baggy trunks and a towel around his neck, would have been him.

CHAPTER FOUR

*S*arah could get used to the beach life. Each morning, Oliver waited patiently as he sat by the bed with his leash, ready for his run. They ran on the sand in the cool of sunrise on a beach empty of everyone except a few truly dedicated shell-seekers and sunrise-watchers. It was addictive.

The dream that had been conspicuously absent since she received the letter had come back to her since her arrival. Each night she added more details to the hazy recollections that had begun to come together. Each day she realized more and more that God loved her so much that He had brought her to this place that He knew made her happy. There was just a feeling she had, that something was going to happen. Good or bad, she didn't know, but something.

She remembered more of the dream every day, and that feeling of something spectacular about to happen showed on her face. Her smile flashed at young and old alike. Avoiding the wedding of an old love was the farthest thing from her mind these days.

SHE WASN'T LATE the day of her appointment with Will Schumaker, the lawyer in charge of the inheritance she had driven over seven hundred miles to claim. The only information she and her father had been able to glean from telephone conversations with him was that they were not the sole beneficiaries.

Driving to the lawyer's office, she had hardly noticed the dense forest of tall, straight pine trees on either side of the four-lane highway that led directly out into the bright sunlight as she crossed the bridge over the Waccamaw River and into Georgetown. Preoccupied by thoughts of what might happen, for the first time since her arrival in South Carolina, she gave little thought to the seemingly easy, relaxed way of life of the residents and tourists along the way.

After the carefree days on the beach, reality had come back to her. Sarah was more nervous than she cared to admit as she tapped on her steering wheel as she entered the city.

"Well, God, here I go to meet my next challenge . . . an inheritance. They've been so closed-mouthed about it. Please take this fear away—fear of the unknown always tries to creep in, and no matter how many times I put it all in your hands, I seem to have a talent for grabbing it back just so I'll have something to worry about. . ."

She pulled into the paved lot of Bodine, Schumaker, and Lentz, Attorneys At Law. When she entered the building through a heavy wooden door, a lady in her mid-fifties with glasses on a chain and huge pink hoop earrings greeted her pleasantly. She was expected.

"Good mornin'! You must be Miss Crawford?"

Sarah bit her lip nervously and nodded. The receptionist got up from her desk and continued. "My name is Carol. Mr. Schumaker is on the phone, but will be right out. He's been expecting you!"

Carol led Sarah into a conference room, brought her some coffee, and left her alone. When he finally joined her, she was stunned to see the balding, quintessential southern lawyer, complete with seersucker suit. She had come down here to do business with Matlock! Disarmed by the random thought and the smell of Old Spice that made her think of her grandfather, she couldn't help but smile when he held out his hand.

"I'm so sorry Miss Crawford. I had a phone call come in just before you arrived that I had to take." With a pleasant expression and a firm handshake, the lawyer continued. "I'm Will Schumaker." In a conspiratorial tone of voice, he added, "I'm about to become a grandpa for the first time, and my wife just wanted to fill me in on the latest news – we're having twins." Mr. Schumaker had a smile that she was sure nothing could take off his face.

Sarah was instantly disarmed by his Southern charm. "It's nice to meet you. Congratulations on the twins, and believe me, your life will change. You should compare notes with my parents sometime."

"I hope to get the opportunity to meet them. Will any of your other family members be able to come?"

"They weren't able to get away as soon as I was, so they sent me to check things out and then they'll come down later."

"I understand. I apologize that I couldn't tell you more about the inheritance on the phone or by letter, but Alex left strict instructions that only when one of the family members came down in person was I to share the details of the inheritance. Which, I might add, is fairly extensive."

He looked down for a moment as he shuffled papers and adjusted the wire-rimmed spectacles on his nose. He peered at her over his glasses and paused. "I'm sure you're curious as to why Mr. Crawford saw fit to leave his estate to your family."

Sarah's eyes widened as she nodded in agreement. "Frankly,

we're stunned. My dad had heard of him, through my grandfather, but never in any detail. We weren't aware that he was still alive or where he had ended up."

"Alex told me bits and pieces over the years. Seems that his father, Thomas Crawford, decided the family needed to move west, but his wife Alice, your great-great grandmother, was expecting Alex—a later-in-life baby—and couldn't travel. Thomas wanted to wait until spring, but William and Raymond decided to just strike out on their own. Unfortunately, Thomas died not long after Alex was born, and the extended family lost touch with your great-grandfather William and his brother Raymond when Alice died just a few years later. He was raised from about the age of four by an uncle that lived nearby."

"So, Alex was an uncle to my grandfather?" Sarah was touched at the tragedy that had befallen this long-lost relative. To grow up without mother or father, and then to have lost touch with his extended family as well added to the sadness of the story. "Did he ever try to find his family before?"

Will looked down for a moment as he shook his head. "No. He married as a young man, but his wife died in childbirth. He never married again. I understand, from talking to him over the last few years, that for many years of his life he tried to make up for his lack of family by making money. Something he regretted later when he was diagnosed with an inoperable tumor. Alex was a good friend to me. He gave me lawyer business when I was just a young man starting out. What he lacked in family ties, he made up for by helping folks in the community."

Sarah was quiet. She began to have a picture in her mind of what Alex Crawford was like. He was a man without a family, but a man who desired to find them, if too late for himself. It was almost too sad to think that her family would benefit from this man that they never had the opportunity to know.

"I'm sure you'll learn more about Alex when you meet Jared

Benton. For now, how about I let you get an idea of just what this inheritance amounts to."

SARAH WAS in a daze as she followed Mr. Schumaker's Lincoln down Highway 17 in her own car. He had shown her the documents from the search Alex had conducted to find his long-lost relatives, as well as deeds and documentation specific to the real estate holdings they had inherited. There was one particular piece of real estate that was foremost in her mind—a restored 1859 antebellum mansion.

Before they left Georgetown, Mr. Schumaker made a phone call. "I've called his office, and Jared Benton will meet us out there to give you a better showing than I could. He was your uncle's business partner and right-hand-man, and he has run the office since your uncle passed. He's a good fella. Knows what he's about." Will had indicated that if her family entertained any thoughts of selling out of the business or the house, Jared would be an excellent candidate to buy them out.

Alone in her car, Sarah's thoughts ran back and forth faster than she could comprehend. She was glad to have a little time alone to digest all the information she'd been given. Jared Benton was the co-beneficiary of a successful real estate business along with her and her family. He was no longer Alex Crawford's business partner, but a partner with her, her sister, and her father.

We have business partners? Sarah's eyes grew wide as she drove down the Palmetto-lined boulevard. The Crawfords of Summerville, Kentucky, firmly planted in the lower-middle class of farm folks and blue-collar workers with the occasional white-collar management-type, had business partners. Who would have thought?

And if Mr. Benton was as close to Alex Crawford as she

gathered from Mr. Schumaker, how did he feel about strangers from Kentucky coming in and taking a majority share of the property and business he had worked to build for the last eight years?

The road to the house was just off the main road, to the left. They passed some modest homes, and at the end of the road, they pulled into a drive marked by two brick gate-posts, the name "Pilot Oaks" on each, but no house was visible. As they navigated the curves through the landscaped property, a large white house finally came into view in an open area. She pulled her car to a stop in front of the house, then got out and stood, awestruck.

It wasn't quite, but almost was, the house in her dream. The sense of *déjà vu* crept over her as she stood there, unable to speak. Every day since she had been in South Carolina, the dream had teased her in the fog of wakefulness each morning, and today she was faced with the reality of a brick and mortar house instead of a hazy image.

The house of her dream had been neglected, but this house was in pristine condition. The white paint gleamed in the sunlight, and the porches with their rocking chairs beckoned. Sarah drew in a large breath, the smell of the marsh and surf blending to create a heady scent that made her wonder if she had finally found what she sought. The sights, smells, and thoughts this place evoked in her were unexpected, and yet . . .

"This . . ." Sarah's voice drifted into silence as she swept her hand toward the house. Tears filled her eyes, and she simply gestured in place of the words that would not come. She looked into Will Schumaker's face as if to verify that what her ears had heard earlier was what her eyes saw in front of her. It was literally her dream come true.

His voice softened as he saw her tears and the look of utter astonishment on her face. "This is your house—well, yours, your sister's, and your father's. Your family members are the sole heirs of the house and grounds." Mr. Schumaker stood beside her. "Pilot Oaks used to be part of three plantations that reached all the way from the Waccamaw River to the Atlantic Ocean. 'Course it's been sold off, bit by bit, but somehow the various owners managed to maintain some marsh and some oceanfront property, which really adds to the value." He looked at his watch and frowned slightly. "Looks like Jared isn't here yet. I'll let you in, and you can look around on your own 'til he gets here."

A graceful stairway greeted her as she walked through the massive front door. Unlike the one in her dream, the banister on this stairway shone with love and care, polished to a satin finish. She touched it lightly and then walked slowly up the stairs to the second floor. She felt less like a trespasser with each tread, but in her mind, it was more like she had switched identities with someone from a far more blessed walk of life than she had experienced.

The tears threatened once again as she passed through each room, each one more beautiful than the last. She hurried, overwhelmed at the thought that her great-uncle had lived here. He had died here in fact, like many before him. The history and human drama that this house had seen overwhelmed her as she stared at the stained-glass window in the stairway landing.

The lump in her throat took away all thoughts but one. *Thank you, God.*

Sarah made her way down the stairs and was about to begin her exploration of the bottom floor when through the beveled sidelights of the front door, she saw Mr. Schumaker deep in conversation with someone on the porch.

She opened the front door to greet the person that she figured was her uncle's business partner. As he turned, her eyes widened as they came in contact with the deepest pair of brown eyes she had ever seen. Brown eyes the color of dark chocolate, fringed with thick black lashes, dark brows gathered above them. The first time she had seen them, on the boardwalk, they had been relaxed. Friendly.

Why, suddenly, did she feel that those eyes were darkened in anger and not in delight at the prospect of meeting his new business partner?

CHAPTER FIVE

*A*s Jared Benton's eyes registered on the young woman in front of him, his eyebrows went up involuntarily in reluctant appreciation of the sight before him.

She was as pretty as he remembered, and she seemed cautiously surprised to see a familiar face. Or was that suspicion clouding her eyes?

Will Schumaker made the introductions, and Jared sensed that the lawyer was watching the reaction of the two young people in front of him. Since he hadn't told him of their "chance meeting," there was no reason for Will not to think that this was their first encounter.

"I'm glad to meet you, Miss Crawford. I understand you're from Kentucky?" Jared's lips lifted briefly at Sarah. She stared at him with open, honest eyes, her smile faltering as if she was unsure.

He didn't want to like this girl. So, she was pretty. Okay she was beautiful. Pretty didn't mean she's good at business, though. The background checks he'd had run on the family seemed legit, but how much could you really find out about a person unless you really dug deep? This woman—this family—represented a stumbling block to his plans. Even if he had to spend an enormous amount of money to buy her out, it might be worth it to be free of long-distance silent partners who could potentially sink the business.

WHAT WAS WRONG WITH HER? She was not the kind of girl to fall apart when a handsome man noticed her. Somehow, she could not help but respond, amazed at the thoughts and ideas that raced through her head. Was he going to acknowledge their previous meeting? Maybe he would explain it later. But why did her heart feel like it was alternately going to stop and then speed out of her chest? She had always laughed when she read romance novels that described that sensation of melting into a puddle . . . and now she knew exactly what that felt like.

He really might be the most handsome man she had ever seen. His dark, wavy hair was cut short but still slightly unruly. His deeply-tanned face sported a crooked smile. The suit and tie in no way hid the muscular build that told her that he was an athlete or had been in the past. If anything, the suit enhanced the broadness of his shoulders and narrowness of his waist. Taller than she by several inches, yet not overly-tall. Those eyes. . . She forced herself to bring her attention back to the conversation at hand.

Sarah blinked and tried to remember where she had lived her entire life. "Um, yes, the western part of the state."

JARED WAS a person who looked people in the eye, and after the initial contact, Sarah seemed to avoid his eyes completely. It was his fault. He should have mentioned their chance meeting at the beach. Now she'll think I have something to hide. When he finally got her to look at him, she had stammered. He wondered about the brightness of her eyes. Had she been crying?

He decided that their best bet was to get on with the tour. Time enough for true confessions later. He gestured toward the door. At this point, he just wanted to get this over with. The nagging voice was annoying him, and he had a mental image of the "still, small voice" sitting on his shoulder, arms crossed, sighing in frustration.

"Would you like me to show you around the property? Pilot Oaks was the house your uncle lived in most of the time. It was his favorite. I told him, many times, that it was prime real estate for a bed and breakfast, but he wouldn't hear of it. "Liked his privacy too much," he said. "Let the vacationers rent the guest cottages over on North Litchfield Beach." Jared looked down at Sarah and chuckled. "It worked. We made more money on the rentals of the cottages and condos than anyone ever thought possible."

They walked through the graceful rooms that joined one another at the grand hallway of the ground floor, and Sarah seemed to relax. She paused at the grand piano in the parlor and ran her hands across the smooth surface. She leaned against the piano, as if to brace herself, and gazed up at him. When her eyes met his, his gaze faltered. That was when he realized that she had sized him up, just as he had her.

Hazel. Her eyes were hazel.

She hesitated, as if searching for words. "I had a dream about a house much like this, except it was in disrepair, as if it had been abandoned for many years. I always think abandoned houses are sad, in a way." She reddened a little as she glanced away.

Jared twisted his lips and wondered, for a moment, if she was for real, or if the "sweet little girl from Kentucky" act was designed to throw him off guard. "I've always thought so, too. That's one reason I got into real estate. I like to take a house that's been neglected, fix it up, and then sell it so that some family can enjoy it. Fortunately, for our business' sake, that usually nets us a profit." He shrugged slightly, relaxing a bit with this newcomer. Whether this was a good thing was still undecided.

They traversed the house and the grounds near it. When they were finished, Jared and Sarah met Mr. Schumaker in the driveway.

"So, what do you think?" Mr. Schumaker asked Sarah.

"About . . .," Sarah raised her eyebrows.

"About the estate? Do you think this is something you and your family would like to take on, or do you think you might be interested in selling out portions of it to investors?" As Mr. Schumaker spoke, Jared took extreme interest in the expressions on her face. He knew what he hoped would be her answer, but he couldn't be sure of anything at this point.

He was fully prepared to buy out Sarah and her family's assets in the real estate business. Alex should have given Jared the opportunity to buy him out. He could have still left the family some cash—maybe the house. Now he wasn't so sure. What did that old goat have in mind?

SARAH SNEAKED a look in her rearview mirror at Jared standing in the drive as she pulled away from the house. She did a mental review of the past hour in his company. He was friendly, but reserved. He had shared a few stories about her Uncle Alex and how he had loved this house. As he spoke of Alex Crawford, she sensed sadness, but also gratitude and love. Sarah could tell that for him, the house was not the important thing, but the man who had lived here. She had never met anyone in real estate that didn't look first at the brick and mortar, and then at the way a house was used.

She smiled when she remembered what he said about his reasons for going into real estate. "I like to take a house that's been neglected, fix it up, and then sell it so that some family can enjoy it." He shrugged as if to take the focus off him and then seemed to relax with her as they made their way through the beautiful rooms. She still marveled at how much Pilot Oaks was like the house in her dream.

And then there was the beach last Saturday. Did he really not remember meeting her on the boardwalk? There were a few times she thought she caught a flicker of recognition in his eyes. But no. She couldn't blame him. She probably wasn't the kind of girl he would be attracted to. As she drove back to the kennel to pick up Oliver, she heaved a deep sigh. What was she getting into?

"So . . . do you think they'll sell out?" Will and Jared had watched Sarah drive away and then decided Jared's air conditioned office would be more conducive to discussing the situation.

Jared leaned back in the soft leather chair and crossed his ankles on the edge of the desk. He looked up at the ceiling, still unsure about what had happened earlier at Pilot Oaks. "I don't know. I don't think she was prepared for the scope of the inheritance. Did they get no warning about the size of the estate?"

"No. One of the things Alex was pretty strict about was that somebody from the family had to come down here and claim the inheritance. They couldn't just decide from home. They had to come see it firsthand." Will shrugged his shoulders. "Seemed a little silly at the time, but I'm sure Alex had his reasons."

Jared gave the older man a half-smile. Sometimes he forgot Will was his lawyer instead of his friend. "You know, Alex was convinced that he'd been blessed with this fortune to help somebody. He often said that he knew there was more of his family out there, somewhere, and that it was probably the reason God never saw fit to bless him with his own after his wife and child died. I just wish he'd had a chance to get to know them before he passed away."

Will frowned slightly. "I still don't know why he didn't just leave it to you. I tried to get him to see reason . . . to see how hard you've worked to build up the business and make him quite a chunk of change . . . but he was adamant about it. I'm sure these are nice people and all, but how could he know that?"

Jared creaked back in his swivel chair as he found a more comfortable position with his elbows on the arms, his hands clasped in front of him as he thought about that last year of Alex's life and about the letter that he had read the day of his funeral. "Yeah . . . well . . . I was pretty upset when he started the search for his family, until I learned about the tumor. And then I thought he was addled. I mean, it was a brain tumor, after all, and you know how that can affect your judgment. He told me something, though, when I questioned him, that made me think he'd spent a little more time with his Bible and in prayer. He just looked at me—you know, the way he could bore a hole right through you when he wanted to—and said 'Jared, son, I don't know how long I've got, and I don't have any idea if I'll ever see this family that I've paid an arm and a leg to find, but I know one thing: when David hid out in a cave, afraid for his life, he knew the Lord was in control. He wrote this . . . 'Delight yourself in the Lord, and He will give you the desires of your heart . . .' I'm done on this earth, but you're not. My desires are for you now. My desire is not to see you the wealthiest man in Waccamaw County. My desire is to see you with a wife, with kids, and a good life.'"

"Sounds like Alex. What did you take from that?" Will narrowed his eyes.

Jared twisted his lips and pursed them as he leaned forward on his desk. "I think he meant that he wanted more for me than he had," he said, quietly. "Do you think it was an accident that I hooked up with Alex when I was sixteen? God works miracles in stranger ways, Will. Alex taught me that a long time ago."

Will shook his head. "I never did understand the connection between you two. Alex never took any interest in kids until you happened along."

"Yeah, well, I guess I stumbled on him at the right time. Dad was part of a major military operation, but I couldn't know that at the time. I was pretty mad that he seemed too busy to spend time with me, and somehow, Alex and I just clicked. For all that Alex was a strange old bird, I like to think we understood one another pretty well." Jared sighed, weariness coming over him.

Will got up from his chair, looked at his watch, and said, "Well, I'd best be headed home. Betty will have supper on the table in about an hour, and I'll have to hear all about the twins again, I'm sure."

Jared noticed that the grin on Will's face had been more "on" than "off" ever since he first heard about his daughter's pregnancy. He smiled and stood up to walk Will to the door. "Tell your daughter congratulations for me, Will. I can't wait to be able to call you 'grandpa.'"

"Me neither, boy. Let me know how it goes with Miss Crawford tomorrow, will you?" His face was somber.

"Will do. Hey, if they decide they don't want to deal with it, I'll be ready with my checkbook." Jared quirked an eyebrow at Will's look of relief.

Will nodded and shook Jared's hand. "Just be careful. You don't know her, and just because she's some long-lost relative of Alex's doesn't make her trustworthy."

"Got it. I'll be careful."

Will waved his hand in dismissal when Jared started to follow him. "I know the way out."

Will whistled on his way out the front door, prompting Jared to chuckle to himself as he sat back down in his chair. He sobered. The staff had gone for the day, and he was alone in the building. He stared at the ceiling and shook his head, then made himself sit back in his chair and relax. He prayed a simple prayer.

"It's over to you, God."

He felt a peace that he hadn't felt in a while. He closed his eyes and felt his muscles relax for the first time that day.

"Delight yourself in the Lord and He will give you the desires of your heart . . . I'm in for some of your educational experience, aren't I, God? It's not about the money. It's not even about me, is it? I know, I know. You'll tell me in Your own good time. I guess I've waited this long to know what you have in store for me, I can wait a little while longer."

Opening his eyes, he stared through the rear window, absently focusing on a clump of pine trees. Sarah Crawford was different from the girls he usually noticed - pretty, sure, but not blatantly so. And the way her longish brown hair blew in the breeze on the front porch, and the blush of new freckles that graced her slightly upturned nose . . . His lips turned up in a smile.

What color were her eyes again? Blue? Green? A little of both, maybe? Then he remembered – hazel. He would look at them carefully tomorrow. Tomorrow might be the last time he would see her . . . and then he caught himself. His brows furrowed as a thought struck him.

He hoped it wasn't the last time he saw her.

Where did that come from? No answer. Just utter quiet.

He would just have to wait . . . just like he had waited for his life to settle down for the last ten years. Did he trust God to know what was best for his life? Did he have the patience that Alex had in the last years of his life, to content himself with the accumulation of wealth, to wait for the partner God had for him, or to perhaps spend the rest of his life alone to leave his fortune to unknown relatives?

There was only one way to learn patience. It had to be wrung out of you. God had certainly been patient with him. Maybe it was Jared's turn to show patience with God.

CHAPTER SIX

$\mathcal{T}$he drizzle that had started before dawn had cleared by the time a nervous Sarah made it to the offices of Crawford and Benton Real Estate on the main road that ran parallel to the beach. When she walked into the lobby, her shoulders eased down, and her lips curled into a thankful smile. She was struck by the décor. Comfortable. Contemporary, but warm.

Her smile was reciprocated by the young receptionist. "You must be Miss Crawford? We've been looking forward to meeting you." The red-head stood and spoke with a slow Southern drawl.

"Yes, I believe I have an appointment with Mr. Benton?" Sarah looked around. "This is a lovely office."

"Thank you. We're very happy here. Oh, and I'm Carla Weaver." She smiled as she took Sarah's hand, but then her face crumpled a little as she shook her head. "We're still not over the death of Mr. Crawford. Were you close?"

"No, I had never met him. From what I've learned about him, I think I missed out." At that moment, a door opened to the left, and Jared Benton stepped out, charming, as usual.

Struck once again at the expressive eyes of this man, Sarah was glad she had opted for the outfit she wore. After a quick look in the full-length mirror before she left the condo, she knew that the lightweight pink cotton dress and strappy sandals were the perfect foil for her newly-acquired tan and what she liked to consider shapely legs. In direct contrast, the light grey suit with white shirt and light blue tie set off Jared's tanned skin and muscular build beautifully.

"Sarah. Good to see you." He shook her hand and held it a little longer than the average shake. When he let it go, she noticed surprise on his face as his eyes met hers briefly. His eyebrows quirked up and the tips of his ears turned a shade pinker. He took a deep breath. "Are you ready to delve into your inheritance?"

"That sounds scary. I've been instructed by my family to look it over and let them know what my 'gut' tells me." She laughed as she felt a blush rise on her cheeks that matched his. For some reason, she suddenly felt like an awkward teenager.

"Well, I thought we would start here. I'll show you around the office and explain the properties and how they work, show you some financial statements and how your uncle and I had our partnership drawn up. By then, your 'gut' should have told you that it's lunch time." He led her into his office and gestured toward a chair. "Have a seat."

"The offices are beautiful. I love the way you have them decorated." Sarah rubbed the arms of the comfortable leather club chair where she sat and looked with pleasure at yet another well-designed room.

"Thank you. I got my way on this one. I don't know a lot about interior design, but I know I like things to be comfortable, and I know what I like."

"I think some people just have a knack for decorating."

"I wouldn't know about that. Somehow it just worked out well. Your uncle, on the other hand—as much as he knew about real estate and what sells—tended toward the stiff and formal in his décor." Jared laughed as he told Sarah about the way he had had to finagle Alex to get him to agree to the overstuffed furniture as opposed to the horsehair sofas and antique pieces that would have been the choice of the older man. "Alex told me that in his day, people wanted to buy real estate from someone who looked successful, so you staged it with the fanciest, most expensive stuff you could find. I finally convinced him that people wanted to be lulled into business these days." Jared raised his eyebrows. "He liked those chairs, too."

Sarah joined in his laughter at the picture he'd painted of the man that was blood relative but unknown to one and a beloved, valuable mentor to the other. Jared suddenly had a faraway look in his eyes and seemed to shake himself to come back to the present. When he looked up, he tilted his head as he met Sarah's quizzical gaze.

"Your great-uncle was like a grandfather to me." A sad look crossed his face. "I grew up a military brat. We never lived close to family, and we were never in one place long enough to make many friends outside the military."

"How did you come to go into business with my uncle?" To call Alex Crawford "my uncle" seemed to come naturally, even though she never met the man – never even heard of him until after his death.

"I met Alex when I was a teenager. My dad was stationed at Charleston Air Force Base, but after nearly twenty years of military bases, he was tired of it. He decided, for once, to think about his family and commute to Charleston to work and live here like normal people rather than have us surrounded by barbed wire in base housing." Jared's lips quirked briefly as he shared the memory.

"So, you've lived several different places, then? I noticed that you didn't really have much of an accent." Sarah was interested in what made this man tick. He had a great sense of humor, great sense of style, and the brown eyes certainly don't hurt, she thought.

"Yeah. I went to high school here, so this is where I call home. I guess the military lifestyle trained the accent out of me. We lived down the road from Alex's estate, and one summer I mowed the lawn for him – my first job." He glanced up. "I guess you could say I know every inch of that place." The shrug, coupled with the boyish grin on his face, made Sarah smile back. She couldn't help it.

"Sounds like you made quite an impression on my uncle, for him to eventually make you a business partner."

"I worked for him in the summers while I was in college, maintenance on the rental properties. I socked back quite a bit those summers. The break before I graduated from Clemson, I still worked for Alex, but a buddy and I invested in a beat-up beach house, fixed it up, and then we had our own rental property. The next summer we bought a couple more. I guess the rest is history." Jared reddened a little as he shrugged again. He seemed like a man who preferred not to focus attention on himself. In her limited experience, men who were this successful tended to want to talk about themselves. What drove him? Where was the chink in his armor? Surely he wasn't as modest as he seemed?

"Enough about me. Do you like education? Will said that you were a music teacher in the town where you grew up."

Sarah twisted her lips in a rueful grin as she flashed her eyes toward him. "It has its moments. I love the music, but sometimes a career in education in your hometown is a mixed blessing. I get to teach alongside people who taught me, which in some cases is great, but in some cases, they have a hard time with the idea that I'm a qualified teacher, just like them." Sarah laughed, more relaxed than she thought possible in this situation.

"I know what you mean – some of the people that work for

me used to be my bosses. It generally goes well, but it's taken some time. I guess when I turned thirty they knew they could trust me."

He showed her the books and the catalogs of the different properties owned by the real estate enterprise. After a few hours, Sarah lifted her head, definitely on information overload. In a short amount of time, she had learned that this was literally a multi-million-dollar business. Jared owned forty percent of the business, Sarah and her family sixty percent, or twenty percent each for her dad, sister, and herself. Even hearing the numbers, she couldn't yet fathom exactly what the worth of this inheritance was.

"Alex didn't want to give up his edge, so he never would sell me more than forty percent. I asked him a few years ago about buying out part of his portion, but he wouldn't go for it. I guess I understand how he felt. I'll probably be the same way when I'm in my eighties." Jared hesitated, and looked as if he would like to ask her something, but instead he just gave her that half-smile.

"Are you hungry?" The question interrupted the many thoughts crowding her mind.

Sarah checked her watch. It was already 1:30, and it seemed like she had just arrived. "Starved." She was surprised that her usually healthy appetite hadn't given her signals earlier.

"I thought, if you'd like, we could pick up some take-out and have a picnic at Pilot Oaks. The grounds are lovely this time of year, and I didn't have a chance to show you the summerhouse yesterday when we were there." As Jared spoke, he slid a laptop and portfolio into a briefcase. "After lunch, I can drive you around to see some of our rental properties."

"That sounds great. I do appreciate the time you have taken on this – I hadn't expected to take your whole day. I know you're a busy man."

Jared twisted his lips and quirked his eyebrows at her. "What are business partners for, if not to help one another make the best of the business?" He stopped and placed his hands on his desk, then leaned toward her. "After all, it's not every day you go from a partner who's a ninety-year-old man to one who is an attractive young lady." He picked up the laptop case and extended his arm to escort her out of the office.

When he loosened his tie on the way to his SUV, Sarah wondered a bit about the wisdom of so much time alone with him. His slightly flirtatious manner threw her just a little. What were his expectations? His reputation was still unknown, and while she wasn't exactly in the first blush of youth, her experience was somewhat limited in the ways of strange men. She knew nothing about him other than what Mr. Schumaker had said. As they left the building, he glanced down at her with a relaxed smile, seeming to envelop her in his warm, brown-eyed gaze. She gazed back, but she had to wonder if he was sincere or playing games with her. Did he really not remember last Saturday?

Relax and enjoy yourself. He doesn't seem like an axe-murderer, does he?

A slight chuckle escaped her lips, and when she looked at him, she noticed that he had quirked an eyebrow at her. When she put her hand on the strong arm that he held out to her, he wore a pleasant, yet wondering, expression on his face. Was he anticipating the afternoon as well, and was he, perhaps, just as nervous as she?

CHAPTER SEVEN

"I couldn't eat another bite." Sarah groaned an hour later as they gathered up the remains of the picnic in the summerhouse. "I'll be running this off over the course of the next few days."

"Seriously? I figured you were one of those girls who could eat anything and never gain an ounce."

"Well, so far, so good. But from what my mom tells me, this metabolism doesn't last forever. Good lunch, though. You can't beat fried chicken and mashed potatoes."

"I kinda thought KFC might be a good choice, seeing as how you're from Kentucky and all." Jared laughed as he put the trash in a bag to take back to the office for disposal.

She hadn't known what to expect by way of lunch and was taken a bit off balance when a bucket of chicken appeared in the picnic basket. Once the bag of garbage was tied shut, they sat in a companionable silence as they looked out over the marshland.

"You realize, of course, that you can now get KFC in China." In the aftermath of the heavy meal, Sarah was relaxed enough to tease.

"I had heard that. Just so you know, I usually do much better than this on a picnic. I . . . hadn't planned until this morning to bring you back out here." He sat there a moment, just looking at her.

The heat and buzzing insects were lulling Sarah into a daze. She turned her head lazily to look at him, finding him studying her as she was him. She tried to read his face, his thoughts, to figure out what his motives were. How did he feel about a family from a small town in Kentucky who could come in and claim majority status in the business partnership that he had built with Alex Crawford? Why would he want forty percent of a business that probably should have been his at one hundred percent?

"Take a walk? I want to show you the swing."

"Swing?"

"Yeah, it's a double swing, like a porch swing, looking out on the marsh. It was coming apart when I started working for Alex, but he let me fix it."

They walked down the path from the summerhouse, and hanging from a huge live oak tree just before the marsh began, there was, indeed, a swing, complete with backrest.

Sarah was entranced. "Oh, Jared . . . This is great." While in complete repair, she could tell from the wood and hardware that it was very old. "I can imagine girls in billowing white skirts swinging on this, not a care in the world."

"You don't see many of these, that's for sure. Care to try it?"

"Try and stop me." She sat on the seat, her left hand holding to the chain. "You're welcome to join me."

"Don't mind if I do. Nice, huh?" He settled into the seat.

Every time she turned, there was something magical around the next corner. She could imagine coming out here to get away from the cares of the day. Did Alex used to come out here to think? Did Jared?

She turned toward him to see him looking out over the marsh. Yes, this was a favorite spot of his, she could tell. "So, you told me that you went to high school here? Do your parents live close by?" Sarah wanted to know more about this man. If she were going to be partner or competitor, she needed to know what drove him.

"No. When I was in college, my dad accepted a promotion that took him to the Pentagon, where he retired. I went there for my breaks that year, and as much as I love DC, it just wasn't home. I loved to work for Alex in the summers, and Tom and I had started our side business with house flips in our off time." Jared kept the swing going, gently, with a mere touch of his foot to the ground.

"Tom?"

"Tom was a buddy from high school and college. Actually, he's still a good friend."

"Still in the business?" The circle of people around Jared was widening.

"No. He's a detective with the police force. Great guy. You'd like him."

"I'm sure I would. Maybe I can meet him someday. Do you have any brothers and sisters?" Sarah wanted to get a picture of Jared's family life. What kind of little boy had he been? Had those dangerous eyes gotten him in trouble or gotten him his way more times than it should?

"I have a brother and a sister, both married. They despair of my ever finding 'the one.'" He rolled his eyes. "My little sister got married about two years ago. Her husband is in the Air Force, stationed in Hawaii. Mom hoped she would fall for a nice accountant or something." Jared laughed. "Anything to keep Jessie close to home."

"Sounds familiar. I get fixed up with every single teacher or quasi-professional that comes within a fifty-mile radius."

Jared chuckled.

"My older brother and his family live in Baltimore, which makes my parents happy, since they're the ones with the grandkids. My nephew is five and my niece is two. They're pretty special kids. I try to get up there every couple of months. If I don't, I don't recognize them, they grow so quickly." Jared shook his head. He pulled pictures from his wallet to show Sarah the tow-headed boy and dark-haired beauty that was his niece. Those eyes must be dominant, she thought as she noted the resemblance of the children to their uncle. It was obvious that family life appealed to him. Why hadn't he found "the one?"

"What about your family? I know you live close to them, but what makes up your family? I know you have a sister. Older or younger?" He had turned the tables on her.

"My mom and dad live in Summerville, like me. Dad is a retired construction salesman, Mom a homemaker. Dad still fills in for the guy who replaced him when things get rushed, like they are now. My sister, Susan, is older than me – married to a wonderful man, Mike Harris. They have two-year-old twin girls, Abigail and Trudy, who are the lights of our lives. Mike is an accountant, and my sister works for an online-based business from home, while she raises her kids. I guess Mom had better luck with Susan than your mom had with your sister on the search for an accountant to settle down with." She shook her head. "Personally, I don't think you could blast them out of the county at this point."

"Is that why you came down by yourself?" Jared spoke quietly, his head tilted. "Can you be 'blasted' out of Summerville?"

She gazed at him, and his eyes seemed to hold her in place. "I guess I really hadn't thought about it. I love my home, my friends, and my church, but lately I've felt a little antsy, like there was more out there, you know?" Why she had told him this? She had just met the man yesterday. My mother would be appalled! She laughed aloud as the thought crossed her mind, then looked away in embarrassment.

"Yeah, I know what you mean. I love the business, love the

area, but . . . let's just say I know what you mean . . ." Jared's voice trailed off.

As she drove to the kennel not far from the condo to pick up Oliver, Sarah thought about her life. She had dated some, but never very seriously. She had had the token prom dates and a steady boyfriend for a short time in college, but somehow it always just fizzled out before it ever went very far. Friends and family had tried to set her up with their friends and family members, but nothing had clicked. Never desperate enough to seek companionship in the wrong places, she preferred to think she possessed some discernment when it came to relationships. Then Marc had come along. The one she thought was "the one." Had she ever been wrong! Was there something wrong with her? If, as her mother and sister believed, there was someone out there for everybody, then where was hers?

A pair of brown eyes flashed in her mind. Jared Benton. Sarah pondered over the day they had spent together, trying to think about him objectively. He was a nice enough guy – extremely handsome in an obvious sort of way. Not usually the kind of man I would have the opportunity to date – not that there are any men like him back home. She chuckled to herself when that thought popped into her head, unheeded.

She jumped as her cell phone rang. It was Dad.

"Sarah, how's it going out there?" The concern in his voice was evident, even over the phone. No doubt he was worried about her, so far from home with only Oliver for company. I'll always be his little girl, she thought with a sigh.

"Everything is fine. I left Ollie in a kennel today while I met with Jared Benton. I didn't figure an active young dog would be too welcome in a place of business." After so much introspection, it felt good to chat with her dad.

"So, what did you find out about the inheritance?" He subscribed to the theory that if something sounded too good to be true, it probably was – and this sounded like a case in point. Things like this just didn't happen in this family. They'd had their share of hard knocks and had learned to accept them. Sometimes it was easier just to accept that things wouldn't go your way in order to avoid disappointment. That was the Crawford way, and Sarah had learned it at an early age.

"Dad, I really think we've fallen into something good. Jared – er, Mr. Benton – showed me the books, talked to me about how he got in business with Uncle Alex, and drove me around to show me some of the rental properties that the real estate firm owns. It's legit. Hey, would you believe that the house we rented a couple of years ago was one of the ones owned by Crawford and Benton?"

On their tour of properties, they had driven past the house. She had exclaimed, "Oh! That's the house we stayed in for our parents' anniversary!"

He had chuckled. "It's a shame Alex didn't know about you then. You probably would have ended up at his house."

"Dad." She came back to the present as she pulled into the paved lot of the kennel. "It would be great if you could all come down here so we can make an informed decision about what to do with this opportunity. I've been told that there are parties willing to buy out our interest in the business, but I'm not convinced that's what we need to do." She bit her lip as she waited for his answer.

"Have you prayed about it?" Dad was discerning. He knew what questions to ask.

"Have I ever! I've run with Ollie on the beach every morning. Today my Bible verse was from Psalm 37 – Delight yourself in the Lord, and He will give you the desires of your heart – I trust Him to tell me what those desires are."

"That's the best you can do then. I'll call you later tonight and let you know when we can get down there. It may be that we can at least come down for a long weekend."

"Thanks, Dad . . . I miss all of you, but the down-time has been nice. I think it's been good for Ollie and me to get away, to be able to think, pray, and just be!"

"Well, we've missed you around here, but I'm glad you're enjoying yourself. I think your mom has been a little worried."

"Mom has, or you have?" Sarah laughed as she heard her dad chuckle.

"Well, maybe a little of both. Be careful, and I'll call you after a while."

"Sounds like a plan. I'll talk to you later."

"All right sweetie. Love you. Praying for you."

"I know . . . Love you, too!"

As she ended the call, she got out of the car and walked toward the entrance of the well-kept kennel area. She could hear his happy bark the minute she entered the yard.

As she got to the gate, Rainey Thompson walked toward her, leash in hand. Her blond curls bounced, and she laughed as she followed one very excited dog that was pulling with all his might to get to Sarah. "Hi, Miss Crawford! I think he's glad to see you!"

"I hope he wasn't any trouble, Mrs. Thompson" Sarah gave Oliver a good rubdown as she took the leash.

The older woman pushed her chin-length hair out of her face and shook her head good-naturedly. "Goodness, no – and call me Rainey – everybody does. He's had a good time, I think. He and my Bongo seemed to hit it off really well." She indicated the terrier mix that had come to sit by his mistress.

"Call me Sarah, please. How long have you owned your business, Rainey? You'd have to be a major dog-lover to do this every day." Sarah noted the clean kennel cages, brightly-colored storage bins that held dog toys and color-coordinated bowls for water and food in each kennel. There was nothing lazy about Lazy Acres Kennel.

"I've done this about ten years, ever since my husband retired and we moved down here. We had vacationed here and just fell in love with the place." Rainey's welcome exuded from her. "How long do you plan to stay in the area?"

"That's a good question. I've inherited a house and some land down here – well, me, my sister, and my dad. We were down here a couple of years ago on vacation and fell in love with it, too. Oliver's become quite fond of taking his walks on the beach." The dog barked in agreement.

Rainey's look brightened. "Crawford . . . you're not related to Alex Crawford, are you?" At Sarah's nod, she went on. "He was a good man . . . so that means you've met Jared Benton?"

"Yes. In fact, we've spent the day looking over my uncle's estate. It's . . . a little overwhelming."

Rainey narrowed her eyes a bit and said quietly, "Sounds like you've got some decisions to make. Well, Bob and I will put you on our prayer list. I'm a firm believer that you don't wait to pray when things are bad. You've got to pray for right decisions in the good times, too!" Rainey's smile broadened when she saw a look of recognition and appreciation flit across Sarah's face.

"Thank you." Sarah held out her hand, which was taken and squeezed. Tears began to prick behind her eyelids. "That's just what I needed to hear."

"Listen, if you're involved in business down here, be sure to bring Oliver over any time. Like I said, he and Bongo got along really well, and he likes repeat visitors! We get a revolving door of dogs for him to play with most of the time, and when he sees a familiar face, it tickles him, no end!"

"It's a deal. As obedient as he is, Ollie's a little rambunctious for some of the things I have to do. I'll call you before I come, to make sure you've got room for him." Sarah didn't want her to think she would take advantage of her good nature.

"That's fine, but not necessary. Listen, we go to church over at Calvary—the big brick church right on the highway between North Litchfield and Murrells's Inlet. We'd love to have you visit with us this Sunday." Rainey walked with Sarah as she gathered Oliver's things to take her leave.

"Thank you! I'm not sure when the rest of my family will arrive to check things out, but I may take you up on that. I appreciate the invitation. Everybody has been so warm and friendly to me."

"That's what brought Bob and me back, year after year, until we finally decided that the grandkids could visit us here as easily as they could visit in Tennessee – and Tennessee doesn't have a beach." Rainey and Sarah laughed as they arrived at Sarah's car. Rainey reached out for Sarah's hand. "Listen, if you need somebody to talk to, come over any time. Don't let yourself get lonely. It's hard to make good decisions when you're lonely, because then you let fear and uncertainty do the thinking for you."

Sarah looked at her, tears almost at the surface again as she realized that it was no coincidence that she was sent to this kennel, at this time. She squeezed Rainey's hand. "Thank you, Rainey. I'm a big girl, but it's kind of nice to know I have somewhere to go if I need help. I'll definitely keep the church service in mind, and I'll probably call you soon." Sarah got into her car, put it in gear, and waved at Rainey as she drove off.

CHAPTER EIGHT

*S*arah couldn't drag her eyes away from the waves that crashed to the shore just over the dunes that lay below the balcony of the condo. She and Oliver had rested from their run on the beach, and her book was still open in her lap to the same page she had been reading half an hour ago. The gentle roar of the surf lulled her with each wave.

She startled, deep in thought, as her cell phone rang. "J Benton." She felt her lips go up in a grin when the caller-ID flashed to life.

"Hello?" Sarah answered, tentatively.

"Sarah, this is Jared."

"Hi. Um . . . how are you?"

"Good. Ah, Sarah, I know we spent the whole day together, and you're probably ready to see anybody but me, but I thought . . . if you're not too tired . . . well, would you like to go out to dinner . . . with me?"

Sarah almost laughed at the nervousness she heard in his voice. What did he have to be nervous about? As she spent time with him today, she couldn't help but notice that when Jared turned his attention upon a member of the opposite sex, there were casualties all around. She shook her head. He didn't even realize. Business. That's what this is about. Why would he be interested in an actual date?

"I would love to go to dinner, and I'm sure there is more business we need to discuss." She spoke as primly as she possibly could.

"I make it a habit to talk about business during business hours and enjoy myself during dinner."

Sarah blinked as she struggled to think of a comeback for that. Oliver. What would she do with her dog? She would ignore his comment about enjoyment. Just thinking along those lines was confusing enough. "Do you think my dog would be okay to leave here in the condo?" Her question was met with a brief pause on the other end of the line. Jared had probably reconsidered his invitation. Just as well.

"Tell you what, why don't we bring your dog with us? There's an outdoor dining area where I'd like to take you, so he should be fine. Then afterward, maybe we could take a walk on the beach?" It seemed as though Jared had it all worked out. "Besides, I would like to reacquaint myself with Oliver."

So, he did remember. This was his way of letting her know he wasn't going to ignore their first meeting. A take-charge guy, huh? Sarah didn't want him to think he was in total control. Not yet, anyway. "This outdoor dining area doesn't have anything to do with cardboard buckets in picnic baskets, does it?"

"No way. I told you – that was the result of lack of intuition on my part." Sarah went weak when his voice became tender. If she reacted like that while talking on the phone, what would happen to her equilibrium if he talked to her like that in person?

"Thank you, Jared. I appreciate the time you've taken to show around a stranger. Would you like me to meet you somewhere?" Sarah tried to make this as much of a business dinner as possible. She would admit to herself, and herself only, that she was beginning to get a little lonely on this solitary trip.

But as for Jared becoming more than a business partner? She had no expectations. She had used up her expectations on Marc. Look where that left her.

"No, I make it a practice to provide all transportation for my dates, thank you very much." She could hear the smile in his voice. "And I don't usually take pity on perfect strangers . . . I'll pick you up at 6:30. I've made reservations for 7:00. You're in Sandpiper 402, right?"

"Oh." Sarah wasn't sure what to say to that. "How did you know?"

"You are in a Crawford and Benton building, remember?" He laughed. "And, I forgot to tell you what my dad did in the Air Force – he was in Intelligence."

When they ended the conversation, Sarah sat there a few minutes and thought about the evening before her. He called her "his date." She gave Oliver a quick hug and jumped up when she realized that her watch said 5:30. "Ollie, I've got to get a move on if I plan to be beautiful in one hour."

SHE WAS ready about five minutes early for her date with Jared. She had selected an outfit that would do double-duty for both dinner and a stroll on the beach. The mid-length navy linen skirt and white sleeveless blouse were dressy enough with a light sweater and casual enough that she could pull off the sweater and catch the warm breezes of the ocean. The strappy sandals were easily removed for a stroll on the beach. She had pulled her curls up in a messy bun that wouldn't be destroyed by ocean breezes.

Oliver sat obediently by her side as she stared at herself in the mirror. "I don't know, Ollie. Maybe I'm not dressed up enough. Maybe I should be more business-like. He didn't say where the restaurant is, just that there is outdoor dining, and then we would take you for a walk on the beach. It still might be a dressier place than this." A ring of her doorbell shook her out of her thoughts and moved her toward the door.

When she opened it, her breath caught at the sight of Jared in casual wear. He stood there as if he had just stepped out of a magazine ad for cologne or something. As she recovered from her initial nervousness, she stifled a giggle as she noticed what he wore – crisp navy pants and a freshly ironed white shirt, open at the collar.

"I take it there is a dress code to adhere to at this dining establishment?" Sarah's eyes danced as she pointed out their clothing choices.

Jared looked at her quizzically, and then realization dawned. "I guess they'll know to seat us together, won't they?" He laughed out loud and then sobered as he looked at her closely. "Does it bother you? I can always run home and change if you want me to."

Sarah laughed and then blushed, thankful for his reaction. "Now that would be silly, wouldn't it? You've only confirmed that I am not underdressed for dinner!"

Should she be grateful or suspicious of his motives? For tonight, she decided to be grateful. This was a nice man.

AFTER A WONDERFUL MEAL at Captain Dan's and a round of miniature golf at one of the many establishments in the Murrells Inlet area, they bypassed the public beaches and drove back to Pilot Oaks where they walked down the boardwalk path to the ocean for the promised walk on the deserted beach with Oliver.

For a few minutes, they walked along in silence until Jared finally broached the subject that they had avoided all evening. "Any word from your family about the business?"

They had stopped to let Oliver off the leash to chase after the waves and eddies. Sarah turned toward the ocean and gazed, almost unseeing, out at the water. It had to come up. This was the point of her trip out here, after all. She felt a slight chill, so she crossed her arms and hugged herself before she gave an answer. He still hadn't mentioned the chance meeting—or was it a chance meeting on the boardwalk? Give it time.

She hesitated before she looked up at him, and when she did, felt her lips curl into an involuntary grin as he indicated the sweater he carried for her, obviously having seen her involuntary shiver. When she nodded, he held it out for her and she slipped her arms into its warmth. "Not really. I talked to my dad earlier today. I think they may to try to get down here for a long weekend to look things over. Susan and Mike's trip to Minneapolis isn't until next weekend."

She felt his eyes on her as she looked back out at the ocean waters. Her thoughts were in as much turmoil as the turbulent waves.

"Well, one thing's for sure; it's not a question of whether you have the inheritance, but what you want to do with it." His voice was soft, and she smiled. His eyes seemed to glow with pleasure when he saw it.

"I guess I still find that hard to believe."

"Believe it."

Sarah nodded. Emotions welled up in her chest. So many decisions. She felt so alone. If she weren't careful, tears would come, and the last thing she wanted was to cry in front of a virtual stranger. And that's what Jared was. He was a business partner, yes, but he was also a man that she didn't know. She was still unsure of herself around him. It seemed, he seemed, too good to be true.

Jared picked up a piece of driftwood and threw it into the edge of the surf, stopping to watch Oliver as he ran toward it. Then he turned his attention to Sarah. "When your family comes, would you like to have access to Pilot Oaks to stay in? I'm sure Will would be glad to help you get set up here for company."

"Would that be possible? I would love for us to be able to stay here for a few days. It would make it so much easier for my sister with the girls." Sarah looked at Jared with a burgeoning hope and a hint of tears in her eyes. She wondered at his readiness to help her so much, and it scared her a little—no, more than a little—a lot. What would a man of his stature want in return? When she looked into his eyes, she didn't see any ulterior motives, but maybe he was a good actor. Maybe he really was that smooth.

He shifted his gaze to Oliver as he pranced and pawed in the edge of the surf and shrugged. "Why don't you call them now, and see if it would work out for this weekend? I'm free this weekend and would be able to show your dad and sister around. Hey, you can help. You've had the orientation." There was a mysterious twinkle in his eyes that Sarah could almost identify as excitement.

She pulled her cell phone out of her pocket and started to scroll down her address book. No time like the present. "I'll do it. I need to see my family again. They need to be here, to help me make some decisions." She shook her head as she got to the number she sought. "It's a little too much right now, you know?" She paused before hitting the call button. "As for the orientation, I probably won't be able to remember anything. I'm on information overload right now as it is!"

While she waited for someone to answer the phone at her parents' house, Jared took Oliver's ball and played fetch with him. Jared laughed and Ollie barked every time the ball went through the air. The beach was empty, except for the three of them.

"Mom? Hi!"

"Hi, sweetie! Where are you?"

"Where am I?" Sarah straightened her spine and put her other hand on her hip in a bit of bravado. "I'm on a private beach down the path from Pilot Oaks, the mansion that Uncle Alex left us . . ."

"Must be nice."

"Yeah, nice work if you can get it." She could feel herself relax as she listened to her mother's voice.

"Is everything okay? I've been thinking about you today. I was afraid you'd be lonesome down there by yourself with only Oliver for company." Sarah could hear the concern in her mom's voice.

"Yeah, Mom . . . I'm okay. It's been a good day. Really, it has. So, have y'all talked to Susan about a possible long weekend?"

"We did, and we're going to try to drive down on Friday and then go back on Monday, if that would work out with Mr. Benton and Mr. Schumaker."

"Great!! I might be able to arrange for us to all stay at Pilot Oaks while you're here. Jared said that it shouldn't be a problem."

"Jared?"

"Jared Benton, you know, Uncle Alex's – or rather our – business partner? We went to dinner tonight, and Ollie's running on the beach . . ."

"Oh, really? So, he's there with you now?"

Sarah tried to keep from rolling her eyes. It was a struggle, but the last thing she wanted was for Jared to guess what her mother was implying. He was pretty discerning. Sometimes uncomfortably discerning.

She glanced over at him before answering. "Yes, Mom, he's been very nice to me. We spent the day going over the business, and tonight he was nice enough to take a lonely stranger out for dinner."

"How nice. I will look forward to meeting him this weekend,

then. I'm sure you're old enough to take care of yourself. You call if you need anything, you hear?"

"I will, Mom. I'll call you tomorrow when I get your accommodations worked out."

"Sounds like a plan. Love you, sweetie!"

"Love you, too, Mama. Bye."

"Is EVERYTHING SET?" Jared and Oliver had come to stand next to Sarah as she finished up the conversation. He had hesitated to ask when he saw her brush a wayward tear from her cheek.

She gave him a bright smile as if to tell him not to ask too many questions. Keep it impersonal. "Yes. They'll drive down on Friday – it's about a twelve-hour drive – and then they won't have to leave until Monday, so they'll have Saturday and Sunday to look around." He watched her face. The more she talked, the more excitement he could see in her expression, and the less distant she became.

"Good. I'll plan to have Saturday and Sunday available for you, if that's all right?" He wanted to meet the family that had suddenly become co-beneficiaries with him of Alex's estate— and, to top it all off, he had almost a feeling of dread that she would decide to go back to Kentucky and never come back. That wasn't an option as far as he was concerned. He didn't know why he felt this way. He just did. Thinking about why would come later.

"That would be great. You have no idea how much I appreciate the time you've given me today. I'll call Mr. Schumaker tomorrow---" She was interrupted by Jared's hand on her arm.

"Don't worry about it. I'll make a few calls tonight and have everything set up for you to move out here tomorrow, if you'd like?" He got out his phone and scrolled through to find Will

Schumaker's number. In a matter of minutes, he had made the arrangements for Sarah to come out to Pilot Oaks the next day before her family arrived late on Friday night.

Sarah laid her hand over his that still rested on her arm. "You're a miracle worker, did you know that?"

She had a pleased and contented look on her face. An unexpected jolt hit him when he realized that with one look at that upturned face he knew he wanted to see that contented expression, wanted to be the reason for that expression, for years to come.

CHAPTER NINE

*J*ared dropped Sarah off at the condo and pulled out his phone.

"Will, it's Jared. Could you give me Mr. Crawford's phone number? I have a little surprise I'd like to give Sarah, if it works out."

"Sounds like you're not exactly getting out your checkbook to buy her out, are you, son?"

Jared shook his head and laughed. He could almost hear the inflection of a smirk on the other end of the line. "No, Will, I haven't gotten my checkbook out. Her family arrives this weekend. She can't make these kinds of decisions on her own, and she's smart enough to realize that. She wants to get their input, and staying at Pilot Oaks might make it a little easier."

"And whose idea was that?"

"Well . . . I guess mine." What had started out as a potential opportunity for him to own the whole kit-n-caboodle had changed, somehow, from the time he saw Sarah's luminous hazel eyes on the front porch of Pilot Oaks.

"You sure about this, Jared?" Will's tone was much more serious this time. "You don't know these people."

"I'll keep my eyes open, Will. Don't worry." He paused. "I think Alex would have wanted me to help them out as much as possible, don't you?"

"Yeah, I guess. I just don't want you to get snookered by pretty eyes and a great pair of legs."

"I think you know me better than that, Will."

"Maybe. Hang on. Let me get that phone number for you."

Jared scribbled the number on a notepad he kept in his car. "Thanks, Will. I appreciate it."

Jared pushed the button to end the call with Will and then took a deep breath, willing his heart to stop pounding as he punched in the numbers and then waited for an answer. "Mr. Crawford? This is Jared Benton. How are you, sir?" He was using his most business-like tone for this phone call.

"Nice to hear from you, Mr. Benton. I understand you've spent the day with my daughter. She spoke highly of you."

Jared smiled in the darkness. He didn't miss the "my daughter" and the tone Sarah's dad used. "That's what I wanted to talk to you about. Sarah's been great. I think she could be a natural at the real estate business."

"Do you, now?"

"Yes, but that's not why I called. I think she feels a little overwhelmed at the decisions she's been faced with, which is why she called tonight. I wondered if you would allow me to arrange for your family to fly out here on Friday? It's only about a two-hour flight as opposed to a twelve-hour drive. You could fly out of Nashville at 11:00 a.m. on a private jet, and then it will be ready to take you back Monday afternoon, and you'll be more rested than you would after a day on the road."

There was a pause on the other end. "Well, I don't know. You have a private jet available?"

"Actually, it belongs to a buddy of mine. I have a boat, and I let him use the boat, and he lets me use the plane. It works out well. What do you say?"

"I think that would be great. I have to say I wasn't looking forward to that drive twice in four days' time. Tell you what, I'll get my bunch together, and we'll be in Nashville before 10:00 a.m. tomorrow. Should I call Sarah to let her know?"

"No." Jared spoke quickly and then modulated his voice down a few notches. "I mean, no, I'd like to surprise her. I'll pick you up at the airport in Charleston and have you back to Pilot Oaks before she even knows what's happened." Jared's plan had fallen into place. He laughed into the phone. "You have quite a daughter, Mr. Crawford." He hadn't intended to say that, but it had just come out. Hopefully Sarah's father wouldn't read too much into it.

"I would have to agree with you there. Call me Robert. I look forward to meeting you. So, 1:00 in Charleston?"

"I'll be there. Thank you, sir. I know Sarah is anxious to see you, and she'll be glad to know you can spend more time here than you'd planned. I'll see you tomorrow!"

Jared ended the call and then made another call to Prudie, the seventy-odd year-old housekeeper who had taken care of Alex's house for the last twenty years, right up until the day he died.

"Prudie? What are you doing with yourself these days?"

"Not near enough, I can tell you," the older woman replied. "What are you up to that you'd call me this close to bedtime, Bright Eyes?"

He laughed at her pet name for him. She had called him "Bright Eyes" since the first summer he had mown the lawn for Alex.

"I've got a favor to ask of you. How's the arthritis?" He hadn't called her in a couple of weeks, and he felt guilty even asking.

Prudie cackled into the phone. "The arthritis is there, but not so's you'd notice. What do you have up your sleeve?"

"Alex's family from Kentucky arrives tomorrow night. One of them, a great-great niece, is already here. I talked to Will, and he didn't see any problem with them staying in the house while they're here – they've inherited it, after all. But you know how big that house is. Do you think if I found somebody to do the heavy work, you could go out there and stay in your old room for a few days, kinda get them oriented to the place?" He hoped that using the same tone he had used as a teenager would get him as far as it used to. Very seldom had Prudie refused him anything he asked.

"I'll do it. I'm not as spry as I used to be, but I do know that house inside and out. You know I never could say no to you, you young whipper-snapper!"

Jared grinned into the phone. He was relieved. It sounded like Prudie was on board. "That's what I was counting on. The Crawfords will be there tomorrow afternoon. I'll bring Sarah over tomorrow morning sometime. Do you think you could come out about 10:00?"

"I guess I could. Sarah, huh? And what is this Sarah-girl like?"

"She's a lovely young woman, Prudie –'nuff said. I'll let you form your own opinions of Sarah and her family. There will be Sarah's parents, her sister and her husband, twin two-year-old girls, and Sarah. Think you can handle it?" He envisioned the huffy look on Prudie's face at the hint of doubt in his voice.

"I think I can, and I will, young man. Don't you get smart with me! I'll be there at 10:00 a.m. with bells on!"

"Thanks, Prudie. I owe you one."

"You owe me more than one, but you're welcome, anyway. I'm anxious to meet this Sarah-girl."

"WE'RE MOVING to the mansion, Ollie. Can you believe it?" Sarah danced around the main room of the condo after Jared had walked her to the door. She gathered her things from around the apartment and prepared for bed at the same time. It was late, but she was keyed up. Her family would be here this weekend.

She snuggled down into the covers and remembered their conversation earlier.

"I'll meet you at the condo around 11:00 tomorrow. Will that be okay? That'll give you a chance to have your run on the beach with Ollie before we take him over to Pilot Oaks." Jared had been talkative on the way back from the beach.

"That'll be great. I can't wait to get over there. Oh, my—a private beach will be great. Jared, I would have never imagined anything like this." Her eyes were round with wonder. "It's almost like a dream, and I don't mean the dream I had earlier. Like a dream you know can't possibly come true – but it does. Does that make sense?" She had rambled, unsure why she felt she could say these things to this man of two-days' acquaintance.

Jared thought a minute before he spoke. "I know what you mean. The first house I flipped and sold, I made more money in two weeks' time than my dad did in a year. You don't forget those things. Being an Air Force brat, you understand pay grades and salaries. The concept of earning as much money as you want just by working a little harder takes longer to grasp. I like to think of it as more of a 'blessing' than a 'dream.' God is good – all the time." He had turned toward her and smiled at her in the dimness of the vehicle.

As she thought back on their conversation, sleepiness stole over her. The fresh air of the evening had finally claimed her and lulled her to utter relaxation. As she thought a bit more about this mysterious man with dark brown eyes, she closed her own eyes to dream a little bit more of what could be.

THE DAY of the move to Pilot Oaks dawned bright and clear, and the forecast for the weekend was more of the same. Sarah and Oliver had their run on the beach as they dodged kids with sand buckets, sun-worshippers, and shell-seekers. "After today, Ollie, we run by ourselves on our own beach!"

It didn't take long to gather her things. The condo had been so well-equipped that she hadn't had to do much more than move her clothes in and put her toothbrush in the bathroom, and she was set. As nice as that was, she was more than excited about the opportunity to stay at Pilot Oaks.

At about 8:30, freshly showered and changed, her phone rang as she put on her make-up. Sarah smiled when she saw the caller ID, "J Benton."

"Hello! How are you this morning?"

She was sure he could hear the grin she felt plastered all over her face.

"I'm great. Did you sleep well? I figure I either wore you out with business or fresh air."

It sounded as if Jared was in a good mood, too.

"I slept like a log. I think the combination of fresh air and the sound of the surf works wonders for tired muscles and over-full brains." Sarah chuckled into the phone, somehow just happy to talk to him this morning.

"Hey, would you like me to pick up groceries for you before you come out to Pilot Oaks? There won't be much there by way of food, I don't imagine, and I figure there will be some things that you know your family will need to have on hand."

Sarah was happy that he offered to do this little thing for her. She had never been treated so well. "Thank you, but I really need to go myself. I'll start a list and run by the store on the way out to the house."

"How about a compromise? Let's get you out to Pilot Oaks, survey what's there, and then you and I can go together? I could show you the best deals in town."

"I can deal with that, and I thank you. I'm sure you have things you have to do. Are you sure you have time to deal with me again today?" Sarah was still in wonder at the time and attention he had paid her.

He laughed. "Don't worry; our business won't suffer if I spend another day with you." He seemed to emphasize the word "our." "Besides, I have my phone, and if any real estate emergencies come about, the office can get me any time." His voice lowered. "Hey, I know you've got a lot to do to get ready for your family, and the least I can do is help you out a little."

Her voice was soft as she spoke. "My parents always taught me not to expect people to do things for me, but to simply say 'thank you' when they do. Thank you, Jared."

"You're welcome. When would you like to go? I'm free anytime. I know we'd said 11:00, but if you'd rather get there earlier, that's fine with me."

"To tell you the truth, I was so excited last night that I packed most of my stuff, and I could be ready in the next half-hour. Whenever is good for you is great for me!" Sarah laughed at her own silliness.

"I have a confession to make, too. I'm close to your neighborhood, now. How about I take Ollie out for another walk while you finish packing, then I'll help put your stuff in your car before we go?"

If she didn't know better, she would think he was as excited as she. "Sounds good. See you in a bit, then!" Sarah ended the call and looked down at Oliver with a smile. "We're on our way."

SARAH FOLLOWED Jared's SUV in her little car, and as she drove, she had a chance to look around at the area around Pilot Oaks. A little off the main road that ran parallel to the beach, it was on a road between Litchfield Beach and Murrells Inlet, past the

State Park. On the left, before the turnoff to the house, Sarah noticed a sign that said "Calvary Church."

She turned down Pilot Oak Road and drove past the modest but well-kept homes that were sprinkled here and there with generous lawns and the occasional barn with horses and other livestock.

When she arrived at the brick gate posts of the estate, her excitement grew by leaps and bounds. Whatever they decided to do with the property and the business, for now this place belonged to her family.

Humbled as the reality settled upon her that they didn't deserve this blessing, tears gathered in her eyes as she drove to the front of the house. She sat there a minute and prayed. "Thank you, God. We've done nothing to deserve this. You've given it to us for a reason. We will depend on You to help us know what that reason is!"

Trust me, Sarah.

When she looked up, Jared stood next to the car, a concerned look on his face.

She gave him a tremulous smile as he opened the door for her and helped her out of the car. "Are you okay?" He still held her hand.

"Yes, I'm just still a little overwhelmed at everything that has happened in the last few days. I just stopped for a minute to thank God for all this. I still haven't figured out how it is that we inherited this." Sarah was surprised that she felt laughter and a sob coming to the surface at the same time, and she dug in her purse for tissue with her free hand.

"I know how you feel." Jared looked at her closely and seemed about to say something else, but didn't.

Sarah looked down at the drenched tissue in her hand, alternately smoothing it and wadding it into a ball. "I'm sorry. I don't usually fall apart with virtual strangers like this!" Sarah was embarrassed by her little outburst.

"Don't worry about it." He looked surprised at her comment. If she didn't know better, she would think he almost looked . . . hurt.

After all, they really were virtual strangers, and she had to try to put enough distance between them to make her comfortable.

Jared squeezed her hand and then let it go. He put his hands in his pockets. "Hey, did you notice the white frame house with the big rose bushes in front, about two houses before you got to Pilot Oaks?"

"I did. It was beautiful. It looked like a house that a family would be comfortable in," she said.

He laughed. "I don't know about now, but it used to be. It's the house I grew up in, before my parents moved to DC." A wistful look was in his eyes. "I've watched it ever since I got into the real estate business. I hope, someday, the lady who lives there will put it up for sale so I can buy it."

"Is that Jared the real estate mogul talking or Jared the home-town-boy talking?" Sarah liked this glimpse into his sentimental side.

"Home-town-boy. I admit it." He flushed a little as he sent her a crooked grin. "Right now, I live in a big house on the beach down the road in Murrell's Inlet, but I would move back to that house in a heartbeat. We were happy here. I guess you could say it was the first real 'home' I knew."

He shrugged a little and gave her that half-smile that became dearer the longer she knew him.

CHAPTER TEN

*J*ared handed Sarah the keys to the house, pointing out which was the front door key, then said softly, "Congratulations, Sarah."

She peered at him through misty eyes. "Thank you, Jared. I'm glad you're here." She shifted her gaze to the house, and he heard the apprehension in her voice as she continued. "It *is* an awfully big house, isn't it?"

"Yeah. It's a lot of house. I still say it would make a great B&B, but what to do with the house can wait until the rest of your family gets here." For some reason, he was a little glad that she was in awe of the mansion.

A lot of women would look upon a home like this as their "due," but Jared didn't think Sarah would fit into the self-serving, attention-grabbing category of girls that seemed to throw themselves at him on a regular basis. What would her reaction be to the house he grew up in? He could see her there, at home in the kitchen, sitting on the front porch, climbing the staircase . . .

When she opened the door, tantalizing smells from the kitchen greeted them. Sarah frowned. At her suspicious look, he broke down and laughed. "Prudie, you can come out now. I want you to meet Sarah."

The little woman bustled out from the direction of the kitchen as she wiped her hands on an apron tied over her jeans. She looked from Jared to Sarah and seemed to approve of what she saw.

"Sarah, I had a feeling Jared wouldn't tell you I was here. He's a mess, that one. I'm Prudie Matthews, and I kept house for your old Uncle Alex for the last twenty-some-odd years. Bright Eyes – I'll tell you about that, later," she gave him a sideways glance as his face warmed, "told me that he thought you might need a little help while your family is here. Is that all right with you?"

"Bright Eyes, huh? Ms. Matthews, it is wonderful to have you here."

Jared's face warmed more at Sarah's teasing look.

"Call me Prudie, dear. Ms. Matthews was my school-teacher sister-in-law."

"All right, Prudie. Thank you. I'll admit I was a little worried. I want to take care of it as it has obviously been taken care of. I can be stubborn, but I'm not crazy – I know when I need help."

SARAH SKIPPED up the grand staircase to scope out bedrooms. Each one had had a bath added in years past, so that was not an issue. Susan and Mike would need a bathroom with a tub for the twins. They would bring portable cribs along so that they could be in the room with them for the few days they would be here.

She looked through the rooms with Jared by her side and took in features in each one that she hadn't noticed in the first, cursory, overwhelming look at the house. Each bedroom had a different color scheme and a different theme. There were antiques, but also comfortable chairs and modern mattresses.

The master bedroom was through double doors at the top of the staircase. When she entered the room, she knew that was where her parents needed to be. It was a study in green and gold, with light walls and bright windows with filmy coverings. The bath had a cast-iron soaking tub and separate shower, and two sinks flanked a storage armoire that held towels and linens.

The next bedroom, a large, sprawling affair, was all in blue and yellow. She knew Susan would like that, and it was big enough for the twins' cribs without feeling the least bit crowded.

There were three other bedrooms on that floor, and her eyes lit up when she saw the bedroom in the back corner. A smaller room, it had a full-sized bed covered in white dotted Swiss fabric. The walls were a soft green, and the curtains at the windows were of white gauzy material that she knew would flutter in the breeze when the windows were open. The bath was all in white and green as well, with a shower in white marble with green glass accents. She was smitten. This would be hers.

JARED WATCHED her as she selected rooms for her family and wondered at her choice of the smaller one. The other two rooms that were left were more opulent and much larger, and yet she chose this one.

When he asked her about it, she looked up at him and laughed. "This is the room I would have died and gone to Heaven for when I was ten! Of course I picked the most girly room. Let's go get my stuff so we can explore the rest of the house."

Sarah skipped down the stairs to the front door. Jared

followed her after he finally came to himself. He caught a glimpse of himself in a hallway mirror and was surprised to see a slightly goofy grin on his face. He chuckled and shook his head. He loved to see her like this. Yes, she was a girly girl, but he also knew she was an athlete, a musician . . . and beautiful.

By the time she was settled in and they had looked into all the nooks and crannies of the upstairs rooms, it was almost lunch time. They had only to follow their noses to the kitchen. Prudie, true to her word, had baked pies and cookies that morning, had a roast in the oven for supper, and had made for their lunch sandwiches of freshly-sliced ham, cheese, and tomatoes she had gotten from a vegetable stand just down the road.

"Is it all right if we eat in here with you?" Sarah asked Prudie's permission but looked at Jared for approval.

"If you don't mind looking at my mess while you eat! I'm not a neat cook, but I clean up after myself." Prudie sat down with them at the large oak farmhouse table.

Jared watched as the two women got to know one another. He knew what Prudie was thinking—any girl that attracted this much attention from Jared Benton must be a pretty special girl. He had certainly had his share of girlfriends and relationships in the past, but here lately he was weary of young, unmarried females who threw themselves at him at every opportunity.

Sarah seemed unaware that she was being watched closely. A few times there was a look of confusion and wonder on the girl's face as she looked up at him, but mostly she seemed to be overwhelmed at the whole situation. When they finished their lunch, Jared suggested they go outside to explore the grounds further. For some reason, he was anxious to show her all his favorite spots on the property.

THE WALK out on the boardwalk over the marshes was an experience like Sarah had never known. She'd been to this area, had seen the marshes, but had not had the opportunity to be actually on the marsh. She stood out where the marsh began to meet the water, and it was like they were a million miles away from civilization. Even though she could see houses, boats, and cars, everything was far enough away that the people were like dots.

"This is beautiful. There is a pungent aroma that is a mixture of good smells and bad, but it's a natural smell, you know?" She wrinkled her nose. It seemed important that she be able to describe the sensation than to simply label the actual smell.

"Yeah, I know what you mean. I've lived a lot of different places – Texas, California, New York, but when I'm out here . . . I'm at home." Jared stood, hands in his pockets, and looked out over the marshland and out to the ocean.

"I can tell." Sarah understood exactly what he meant. "When we were here before, I can't explain it, but I felt that way, too." She gazed at him, wondering if he felt the same wonder she did.

Jared tilted his head and lifted one side of his mouth in silent agreement. He cleared his throat and laughed when he caught her hand. "Come on, there's another place I want to show you before I have to leave for a while." He led her back up the path toward the yard.

"This," he said proudly as he walked her down the beach a little way and through a wooden gate, "is the vegetable garden – or it was, anyway. I used to stand here and pick tomatoes off the vine and eat them – or at least I did when Lester wasn't around. When I started working for Alex, the cook still got vegetables and herbs from here, and there was Lester, whose main job was to maintain it and keep it productive. Alex gave him permission to give away whatever wasn't needed for the house."

"If it was anything like our gardens, and my grandfather's gardens, there was always extra." Sarah told him about the bags of tomatoes and zucchini that would appear on doorsteps and carports in their neighborhood.

"Lester kept the nursing home supplied with fresh vegetables a lot of the summer and made sure some of the less fortunate folks in the area had plenty. Prudie usually helped by canning and freezing, too. The kitchen was my favorite place to hang out back then."

"I can only imagine." Sarah spoke quietly.

"Yeah." He shrugged his shoulders as he looked down at her. "It was a pretty good way to grow up. I'd work around here most days during the week. Prudie spoiled me rotten with cookies and slices of pie every time I showed up at the kitchen door, and then I'd go home and Mom would spoil me rotten there. She thought I'd had a hard day at 'work.'"

"Mom would love a garden spot like this. I hope I have time to bring her down here. Just the idea of having a garden with the breeze off the ocean and off the marsh would be Heaven. One of the garden spots we used when I was a kid was a creek bottom. It was low, between two hills, had no breeze, and bred mosquitoes. I hated that spot." She laughed even as she gave a little shiver of displeasure at the memory.

He chuckled. "I can imagine. I don't know many teenage girls who want to be in a hot, sticky garden in the summertime."

They walked back to the house. He glanced at his watch. "I've got to run for a little while. Will you be okay here?"

Sarah trembled a little when he put a hand on her upper arm. Does he look pleased? And was that a little tremble in his hand, as well? "Oh, I'll be fine. Prudie's here, and I have my faithful companion. I'll walk you to your car." She broke eye contact and bent down to scratch Oliver's fuzzy chin, damp and dirty from digging around the garden area.

"Make sure she doesn't get into any trouble, Ollie, okay?" Jared smiled up at Sarah as he reached down to ruffle Oliver's coat, to which Oliver wriggled happily.

"I still can't get over how much Ollie likes you." Sarah raised her eyebrows. "For a dog who doesn't generally like men outside the 'family circle,' he sure has accepted you."

Jared winked at her as he opened the car door. "Can't help it if he has good taste, now can I?"

"I guess not. See you soon."

"Very soon." Jared raised a hand to wave as he got in the car and drove away.

Sarah waved, then put her hands on her hips and shook her head at Oliver.

CHAPTER ELEVEN

*S*arah wandered around the property, played fetch with Oliver, and began to recognize contentment settling over her at the idyllic setting that was Pilot Oaks. What would it be like to live here full-time? With that question came a million more and along with them the anxiety that prompted her to call in reinforcements in the form of her family.

The responsibility of the decisions she was being asked to make weighed heavily on her. It was one thing to make life-altering choices that affected herself, but her family? On the other hand, she had always been the "sensible" one: obedient and anxious to please, and in general the calm one of her group of friends. When she secured a rare job in her hometown where high school choral music positions didn't come available very often, everyone agreed that she deserved the honor. When she became engaged to the hometown sports legend, it was no more than had been expected.

Good choices were rewarded. Sometimes what everyone thought was a good choice turned out to be heartbreaking instead—but she had never been in a position like this, where her choices would affect not only herself, but also everyone she loved most in the world.

She wished her sister were with her already. She wouldn't have any sympathy for her plight, but she would have been there for her. She would have probably said that if Sarah were married, or if she had kids, she would understand what daily life was like for her – always having to think beyond herself. Yeah, well. Dad and Susan were the ones who decided she should come out here without them. She didn't exactly beg for the opportunity, but, she didn't turn down the chance at a solitary vacation, either.

By about 3:00, she had pulled a yellow legal pad out of her box of books. In the midst of her "Pros and Cons" list, drowsiness came over her as she reclined in the chaise lounge in the backyard, underneath the huge oak tree that shaded most of the patio area. She didn't have a clue if anyone else was around or not. Would Jared make it back today?

"Probably not." She spoke aloud. Her thoughts began to run along the negative as she fought sleep to finish the list. "As much trouble as I've been, he'll probably be glad to see me head back to Kentucky." The pen slipped from her grasp, and she went to sleep, her dreams were a mixture of dark-eyed strangers and confusing images of waves, rose bushes, marshes, and vegetable gardens.

WHEN PRUDIE OPENED the front door to Sarah's family, she laughed. "You have to be Sarah's mother! I've seen resemblances before, but those eyes are sure your legacy!"

Jared looked around, distracted, as he introduced Prudie to Mr. and Mrs. Crawford and the Harris family. "Where's Sarah? I thought she would be around to meet us." Her car was in the drive, but she was nowhere to be found.

"She didn't know when you were gettin' back, remember? She also didn't know you were bringin' her folks this early, so I saw her go out on the patio with one of those big yellow notepads and Oliver." She pointed to the back door. "Last time I looked, she was sound asleep on the chaise lounge, with the dog snoozing right there on the ground beside her. I reckon she's had a lot on her mind these last few days, hasn't she?"

"Oh no," Susan moaned. "Not the yellow legal pad. She's made lists." She shook her head as she shifted a sleepy two-year-old Trudy to her other hip. She looked over at her mother with mock severity. "It's a good thing we're here, Mom. She must be stopped."

Susan's husband, Mike reached out and took the nodding toddler from his wife. "Aw, leave 'er alone, Suze. A little more organization never hurt anybody."

"My husband, the accountant and missing twin of my sister in the Obsessive-Compulsive Department."

Jared had spotted the group at the airport immediately. Prudie was right; Sarah had indeed inherited her mother's large, hazel eyes, rimmed with brown lashes. It was a dead giveaway. And while her sister didn't look that much like Sarah, her mannerisms and inflections had him smiling as soon as they met.

They seemed a little more surprised to meet him than he was to meet them. Apparently, they were under the impression that their old Uncle Alex's business partner was in the same age range as their relative.

He had gone at once to Sarah's father, Robert Crawford. He shook his hand and introduced himself. They seemed impressed that he knew each of their names, and he caught several speculative glances between Sarah's mother Linda and her sister, Susan. It tickled him in a way that was a surprise to him. Usually matchmaking simply served to make him nervous or irritated, but for some reason, this time it just seemed natural. Almost expected.

IN HER DREAM, Sarah walked along a deserted beach, dog by her side, hair swirling in the wind. As she looked over at her companion, she was surprised to see a dark-eyed stranger beside her, his hand wrapped around hers. The pressure startled her into wakefulness.

She lazily opened her eyes and looked directly into Jared's gaze. Her mouth curved into a slow smile.

"Hi." Jared spoke softly, his face close to hers. "I have a surprise for you, unless you'd like to go back to your dreams – they must have been sweet ones!"

She saw the twinkle in his eyes and realized that she was not still in the midst of her lovely dream. Her eyes flew open. She sat up quickly when she saw her family behind Jared.

"Mom? Dad? You're . . . you're all here! How did you . . . what happened to tonight?" Sarah's color was still high from Jared's method of waking her. What had her family thought about that? She shoved the thoughts to the back of her mind to deal with later. Her mind was whirling. They hadn't known each other long enough to have a "relationship." Her family was here . . . they hadn't left her to make these decisions on her own. She jumped up to give hugs all around and stopped only when she, in her excitement, almost hugged Jared as well.

"Hey, I wouldn't mind one, too!" He laughed at the stern look that Sarah attempted to give him. A stern look tempered with a mouth that refused to curve downward.

"You might want to reconsider that hug, Sarah. Jared here flew us all in on a private jet so that we could spend more time here and not be so tired." Her dad laughed at Sarah's embarrassment, then turned his eyes toward Jared standing next to her. His expression was one of assessment. Sarah knew he was concerned for her. He didn't want his little girl to suffer yet another broken heart. "He thought you might need a little reinforcement."

"You did that?" The tears were very near the surface as she crossed over to Jared and gave him an impulsive hug that left them both red-faced and a little startled. "Thank you." She spoke quietly into his shoulder and avoided his eyes and the eyes of her family members.

She came to herself and reached down to pick up brown-haired Abigail, who had stood patiently at her side with her little hands up. The tiny girl opened and closed her hands with the signal they had come to know as "pick me up." After she hugged her niece tightly, Sarah led them into the house.

"I've already picked out your rooms for you. I hope you like them." She still held Abigail with one arm and reached down with her other hand to the recently-awakened Trudy next to her.

Jared stopped short as he paused to helped Sarah's father and Mike with the luggage. She walked slowly and carefully up the stairs, pausing to look over her shoulder, where she saw him staring at her, his mouth hanging open. Dad patted him on the back. "I think the best way to get up those stairs is to take it one step at a time."

Sarah couldn't help but smile to herself and feel a little spring in her step as she made her way upward.

CHAPTER TWELVE

*S*arah sat at the large table in the dining room of the mansion and looked around at her family with contentment. Jared sat across from her and caught her eye. She tilted her head a little as she grinned at him, and he crooked his eyebrow at her. The rest of the family was involved in conversation and the babies, and they didn't notice the silent exchange during the dinnertime talk.

He held her gaze and whispered across the table, "Beach, later?" to which she nodded "yes," the heat rising gently to her face.

Jared plunged into some business talk when the inheritance became the topic of discussion. "Mr. Crawford, I'd love to show you around the real estate business part of Alex's estate tomorrow, if you'd like. There's room for all of you in the van, and I can leave that for you to use while you're here."

"I would like that, Jared – and please, call me Robert. I don't feel right to call you Jared if you don't call me Robert – even if you are young enough to be my son." He looked curiously at Sarah. She looked down to hide the blush that stained her face.

Mom chimed in. "As much as I would love to see everything, I think I would be better off to let Susan and Mike go, and I can stay here and take care of Trudy and Abby. I figure I'll hear all about it, and I don't know one thing about real estate. The girls and I will play outside in the back yard, explore a little—and then in the afternoon they can get a nap."

Sarah spoke up, excited. "Mom, first thing tomorrow, I've got to show you the garden spot. It's down by the marsh, and you even get ocean breezes. Can you imagine what we could have done with a spot like that when I was a kid?"

"Imagine what I could do with a spot like that now." Mom laughed. She looked over at Jared with a chuckle. "Sarah was never a fan of large-scale gardening, especially where we had ours."

"She told me about the one in the creek bottom – mosquitoes and all. Doesn't sound like much fun to me, either." Jared laughed.

Sarah tilted her head. "Hey, one thing about the spot here, if you got tired of working in the garden, you could always run to the beach to take a break."

"We'd never have gotten anything done at that rate." Susan looked at her sister. "Not that you got much done, anyway."

Sarah shrugged. "I guess it just didn't move fast enough for me. That's why I joined the track team. Ollie likes to run with me a lot more than he would like gardening with me."

Jared nodded. "I agree with Sarah. I like the stuff that comes out of the garden, but that's about the extent of it."

The ample meal over, the babies began to show signs of weariness that only a bath and bed would satisfy.

As she got up from the table, Sarah looked at Jared, her eyebrows lifted slightly. He nodded. She turned to the rest of the family. "I need to walk Ollie on the beach while it's still light. Is there anything I can get for you before I go out?"

Her dad looked at her with concern. "Are you sure it's okay to go by yourself?"

"Um, sir, I'll be glad to go with her." Jared reddened slightly. "I'll need to leave pretty soon anyway. That way you all can have some time without me around."

Susan and Mike gathered up sleepy little girls to put them in the tub, and her parents started to pick up dishes to help clean up, much to Prudie's protest. Mom held up her hand to calm her. "I want to see how this kitchen works, and we appreciate the wonderful supper too much to leave you with all this. Besides, I've got some things to ask you." Mom began her inquisition as she followed Prudie to the kitchen with a stack of dirty dishes.

SARAH AND JARED were quiet as they made their way to the beach, an excited Oliver glad to be off the leash to play ball and bark at the crashing waves.

"I like your family." Jared interrupted the companionable silence. She looked up at him pensively, still quiet. He stopped and placed a hand on her arm. Without thinking, he turned her toward him. "Are you okay?"

"I'm fine. I guess I'm still in that 'overwhelmed' mode." The breeze off the beach blew her hair and turned it into a swirl of mahogany silk. "You've done so much for me, and I . . . I guess I just wonder why."

He looked off at the water, then turned back to her and looked down at her hands that he had involuntarily taken into his. He gave her a twisted little smile as he narrowed his eyes a little in thought. She startled slightly when he lifted one of her hands to his lips. "I guess I'm trying to figure it out myself."

PRUDIE WAS OBVIOUSLY proud to show Linda around the kitchen and around the house. They "clicked" immediately. Within an hour, Linda felt comfortable enough with the older woman to ask her the question that had been foremost on her mind since she found out that they were to fly to South Carolina rather than drive the twelve hours it would have taken to get there.

"So, Prudie, what do you know about Mr. Benton? It was so gracious of him to fly us down here rather than have us drive down." She dried the dishes as Prudie washed.

Prudie gazed out over the back yard, still light with the long days of summer. "Jared's a good boy." She fell silent, and Linda didn't push. When the last dish was dried, Prudie motioned for her to sit at the kitchen table and continued the conversation as though she had never stopped talking. "He practically grew up on this place. Started to mow yards here when he was about sixteen. Alex took an interest in him early on. Those bright eyes and quick mind—well, Alex knew a good thing when he saw it. I don't think it took long 'til he decided this was a boy smart enough to teach the business."

Prudie shook her head and looked away, as if she were seeing a scene from years ago. "Prudie, he said, what do you think of that boy there? He asked me that sitting right here where we're sitting today."

Linda tilted her head and looked at her. "What did you tell him?"

"I said, well, I think he's a good boy – still wet behind the ears. He was just nineteen then. He was thinkin' about law school then, or maybe even some kind of law enforcement. 'Bout to graduate from Clemson, he was."

"Jared went to law school?"

Prudie shook her head sadly. "Never made it that far. Started flippin' houses during college to pay his way and so he'd have time to play a little football. My, but he was a strappin' young man. I watched him grow from a boy to man over those summers."

"What changed his mind?

Prudie looked down at her weathered hands on the table. She didn't meet Linda's eyes. "Oh, a few things. It just didn't work out. I remember Alex telling me he just didn't see it. I guess he was right. Jared, cooped up in an office or in a courtroom? Hard to imagine."

Linda chuckled.

"He had a girlfriend back then. I told Alex that he just had to let God take care of his plan for the boy and not to interfere. He worried about him, and I did, too, but I knew God had great things in store, in His good time."

As Jared drove away, Sarah suddenly felt a sense of loss. The walk on the beach had done nothing to quell the restlessness she felt in her stomach. If anything, it simply raised more questions. The thought of a discussion with her family just now was more than she wanted to deal with. Just like this whole situation.

She sat on one of the rockers on the front porch with Oliver at her feet, relaxed after his run.

Lost in her own thoughts, she didn't hear the front door open

"Hey, sweetie." Dad sat in the rocker next to her. "What are you thinking about?"

She paused. "Oh, lots of things, Dad." She didn't quite meet his eyes, but she didn't want to shut him out, either. After a few seconds of silence, she finally decided to broach the subject of the inheritance.

"Dad, I know you'll look at the business part of the

inheritance tomorrow, like I did yesterday, so I don't want to sway you or Susan with my opinion. I want you to keep an open mind when Jared shows you around, okay?" Sarah looked into his eyes as best she could in the dim light.

"That's the plan." He spoke deliberately. "You like it here, don't you?"

"I do. I don't know what it is, but I feel . . . right . . . here." She looked at her father again and shrugged her shoulders before she changed the subject. "Dad, when did Jared arrange for you to fly down here?" Curiosity had finally gotten the better of her.

"He called me last night, said he wanted to save us the twelve-hour drive, and that he had a buddy that could fly us down on his private jet. That was too good an offer to refuse." When Sarah still looked confused, he continued. "He wanted to surprise you, Sarah. That young man seems to think a lot of you on such short acquaintance." She couldn't help but notice the quizzical look on his face.

"He's been so nice to me, Daddy. He was so patient when he explained things. He showed me the office and a lot of the properties and showed me all around this property. He told me about its history and about when he worked here as a kid. And then he goes and does this for you – and for me – so that we could have more time to be together and talk things out. He's made me feel like I'm not alone, you know?" It all came out in a rush. Sarah blushed slightly and gave her father a questioning look. There. She'd said it. She admitted that she was lonely.

"I know, baby. God is good, and He takes care of us when we least expect Him to, doesn't He?" Her dad laughed softly, then took Sarah's hand and squeezed it gently. "We'll see what tomorrow brings, okay? We'll none of us make any decisions until we've had a chance to look everything over and then pray about it. How about we start with that right now?"

Dusk crept onto the property, and the shadows grew long as

father and daughter sat on the porch, hand in hand. They each poured out their hearts to their Heavenly Father, asked for wisdom and guidance, then praised Him for His goodness – all the time.

CHAPTER THIRTEEN

*J*ared escorted her dad, Susan, and Mike on the "grand tour" of the real estate office, much like he had done for Sarah a few days earlier. Sarah followed behind quietly. She took this opportunity to observe the office, the morale of the staff, which was at half-staff on peak-season Saturdays—and Jared's interactions with them and with her family.

Over lunch, this time at a seafood restaurant that overlooked the marsh, Mike asked Jared some questions about the financial end of the business, and her dad questioned him about the housing market in the area. The men were in deep conversation about the deep-sea fishing opportunities when Susan and Sarah left to visit the ladies' room.

"Okay, Sarah, what gives? I've watched you two since last night, and I think there's definitely something going on between you." Susan confronted Sarah as soon as they were out of earshot.

"Susan, surely you don't think there's anything going on between Mike and me?" Sarah made a face of mock-surprise and guilt as she laughed at her older sister.

"Very funny. I mean Mr.-better-looking-than-anyone-has-a-right-to-be Jared Benton! Interesting that you didn't see fit to tell us how young he was when you called home." Susan smiled knowingly, eyebrows arched in question, obvious in the feminine need to find a match for her unattached sister.

"Hey, nobody asked how old he was!" Sarah responded somewhat defensively and then softened as she glanced at her sister coyly. "He is awfully cute, isn't he?"

"That's an understatement," Susan replied dryly.

"I don't know." Sarah looked down for a few seconds and then back up at her sister, eager to find out what she thought about Jared. "From the first time I met him, I felt . . . something. I'm trying to sort things out in my mind, but decisions about this inheritance keep crowding me. I've been burned before. I guess that's why I called you guys to come in as back-up." Her face warmed with embarrassment.

"Well, if the look on his face when he looks at you is any indication, I don't think you're the only one that feels something. An old-fashioned romance novel would definitely call that look 'smitten.'" Susan twisted her lips smugly.

"I don't know how somebody like him could be interested in me, but I don't want to think about that right now. At this point, he lives in South Carolina, and I live in Kentucky. I'm not big on long-distance relationships, and until this thing with the inheritance is decided, I don't want to think about anything but that. Is that clear?" Sarah was serious, and she hoped her sister knew it.

"Okay, okay . . . I won't say another word until this is settled."

They began moving toward the gentlemen, weaving through the restaurant.

"Thank you." Sarah breathed a sigh of relief. "Can you encourage Mom to do the same?"

"I'll try, but I know there's a young man with dark eyes about twenty yards from us that seems to be doing everything in his power to see that you like it here."

"Tom. It's Jared. You busy tonight?" Jared was at loose ends after a day with Sarah and her family. He knew they needed some time to themselves after the overwhelming amount of information they had been subjected to. If the situation was a lot for him to digest, he could only imagine how this family felt.

A detective with the local police force, Tom was probably Jared's oldest friend. They had met on the football field in high school, when Jared was a skinny new kid at football try-outs. Jared was a freshman, Tom was a sophomore. Six inches taller than Jared, he just laughed when he saw that Jared's task was to take him down. He didn't laugh long. He found out quickly that to laugh at Jared Benton meant a quick trip to the ground. After that, Tom had nothing but respect for the slight teen.

"Nope, not a thing. Are you tellin' me that the most eligible bachelor in Murrells Inlet can't get a date for a Saturday night?" Tom laughed. It was a running joke between them that one or the other of them was voted "most eligible bachelor" each year by the Junior League – a title that embarrassed them and that both found distasteful. "I think there's a baseball game on tonight. Wanna come over?"

Jared laughed ruefully at the "eligible bachelor" joke – this was, unfortunately, his year for the title. "Yeah. Want me to bring some pizza?"

"Sounds good. I'll be here, just finished the yard. Some of us don't have 'people' who do that for us," Tom said.

When Jared arrived at Tom's house, he noticed the neat lawn and freshly washed car in the drive. Tom kept his unmarked police car cleaner than most people kept their expensive sports cars. Jared wondered if Tom's clean freak tendencies scared off the very women who thought it so cute when they first came on the scene.

Tom met Jared at the door and grabbed the pizzas as they walked through to the kitchen. "So, what have you been up to? I haven't talked to you since last weekend." Tom pulled plates from the cupboard and napkins from a drawer while Jared put ice in two tumblers.

Jared grimaced and began rubbing the back of his neck. "I've been pretty busy." He didn't know exactly how to describe his week.

Tom watched as Jared poured his Coke into a glass. "Something going on?"

"I don't know. Maybe." Jared shrugged. "I met Alex's family this week – you know, the ones that inherited his house and part of the business?"

"How'd that go? I still can't believe Alex didn't leave it to you. You were like a son to him, after all." Tom sounded a little irritated that Jared wasn't more upset at the legal proceedings.

"Hey, Alex left me something that was better than all the money and property he could ever own. You know that." Jared wanted to stop Tom before he could get started.

"Yeah, well. So, what was this family like? Didn't you tell me they were from Kentucky?" Tom's expression was curious.

"They're nice folks. Just your regular, hard-working people who haven't had things handed to them." Jared chomped into his pizza as Tom turned on the TV.

"How many heirs are there?"

"Well, the inheritance actually goes to Robert Crawford and his two daughters, Susan Harris and Sarah Crawford. Sarah came down last week to look things over, and the rest of the family came down yesterday. I took them around the office and the properties today, and they're staying at Pilot Oaks." Jared kept his eyes on the game as he spoke, but he didn't really see any of it.

The two men watched the game in silence for a few minutes. By the time he got to his third slice of pizza, Jared started to relax a little.

After about four innings of conversation about mundane day-to-day things and current events, Tom looked him in the eye. "So, what's got you worried about the Crawford family? Do you think they'll want to sell out, take the money and run, or what?"

Jared was surprised at Tom's take on the situation. "There's really nothing worrying me about them. I've told them that if they want to sell all or part of their share of the business, I'd be glad to buy them out, but if not, I'd do all I could to help them. Stability is in my best interest as well as theirs."

"I guess you seem kind of preoccupied, that's all. Do you have any idea what they'll decide?"

"I don't know. Sarah . . ." Jared paused when he said her name. When he looked over at his grinning friend, he cleared his throat and deepened his voice as he frowned. "Um, Sarah really seems to be interested in the business. She was the one that came down early. I showed her around on Thursday, after she met with Will Shumaker on Wednesday. I met them at Pilot Oaks that afternoon to show her around the house. Today I took Robert and her sister Susan and her husband Mike around, and they seemed interested, but I think they needed to talk about it amongst themselves tonight." He sighed as he picked up his soda.

"Well, you don't have to look so depressed about it." Tom raised his eyebrow comically and held out the pizza box for Jared to take a fifth piece of pizza and set it back on the coffee table. "I can't wait to meet this girl. She must be special to bring a smile to the face of this year's most eligible bachelor at the mention of her name, and a frown on his face at the thought of not seein' her." Tom studied his slice of supreme pizza carefully and didn't even flinch when Jared threw a newspaper at him.

THAT EVENING Jared made himself scarce. Prudie went back to her house for the evening after her mom assured her that they could take care of themselves for supper with all the leftovers that were still in the refrigerator from previous meals.

They all sat on the patio in back, relaxed after a light supper. Abby and Trudy toddled around, playing with Oliver, who enjoyed every minute of the attention he received.

"Dad, what do you think?" Sarah was the first to broach the subject they had danced around all through the evening meal. She was anxious to hear his opinion. Change wasn't easy for him. He had seemed, as she had, overwhelmed by the inheritance. A business operation on the scale of Crawford and Benton Real Estate was like nothing they could have imagined.

Her dad leaned forward in his chair and looked down for a minute before he answered. "It's an outstanding opportunity, isn't it? I don't know if I'm ready to pull up stakes and move out here yet, but it is tempting to hang on to it if we can, if it's as good as it looks right now. What about you, Susan? Mike?"

Mike nodded. "I've looked closely at the financials and talked to a few of the employees, and I have to admit, I'm impressed. I agree with you that it's a great opportunity if it's something you feel like you want to keep your finger in. Jared told me that if we wanted to sell all or part of the business, he would be prepared to buy us out, but that he wanted to work with us and help us in any way he can."

Sarah was surprised at Mike's take on the situation. He usually tended to be over-cautious, if anything. In this case, he seemed . . . well . . . excited.

Susan weighed in. She played devil's advocate, as usual, much to Sarah's dismay. "Would we be as well off to sell out and invest the money? At this point, we each – Sarah, Dad, and I – have twenty percent and Jared forty percent. That's a pretty big chunk of change. If any of us didn't want to hang on to the business, I'm sure Jared would jump at the chance to buy out any one of us. It would, after all, give him the majority in the partnership." She looked carefully at Sarah.

"Sarah, we haven't heard from you. This was your second look at the business. You've also spent more time with Jared, so you might have a better idea of what he hopes will happen." Her mother spoke calmly. "What does your intuition tell you?"

She had hoped it wouldn't come down to her, but it had. She straightened her shoulders, put on her "game face," and cleared her throat as she looked at each of her family members. She surveyed the house and yard and then down at her "Pros and Cons" list on the table beside her.

"While I was here alone yesterday, I made a list of pros and cons." She rolled her eyes at the chuckles coming from her family. "I know. You think I'm a list-making fool, but it's sometimes the only way I can make sense of things that have to be thought out carefully and objectively. Here is what I came up with:

"Pros—We would own a dream house in a dream location; The income stream from the real estate business would enable Mom and Dad to retire more comfortably; income from the real estate business would enable Susan to be a stay-at-home mom if she chooses; income from the real estate business would enable me to explore other options than education; and on the frivolous side, it gives us opportunities for great beach vacations."

Sarah grinned at that last one when she heard her mom laugh.

"That's always at the top of my "pro" list." Mom gave her a wink and a thumbs-up.

Sarah held up her hand. "It's not that simple. Here's the flip-side," she said. "Cons of owning an old, historic house— maintenance, taxes, utilities, general upkeep; cons of retaining our shares in the business – taxes, relocate or silent partner, no experience in real estate business; and then another thing we haven't ever dealt with before: hurricanes."

Her dad looked thoughtful. The rest of the family was quiet and a little more solemn as she finished. "There's a lot to think about, isn't there? I, for one, think we need to pray about it and sleep on it. Agreed?" He looked at each one as they nodded their heads in agreement. "Do you know anything about the church up the road, Sarah?"

"Actually, I was invited to that church by the lady who runs the kennel where Oliver stayed the other day. I'd like to try it out, if you're all game?" Sarah received affirmative answers, so the plan was set – they would attend the 11:00 a.m. service at Calvary Church on Sunday.

CHAPTER FOURTEEN

*T*he front doors of the church were propped open as people filed into the sanctuary. The strains of the old hymn "Great is Thy Faithfulness" flowed from the piano and organ, barely audible over the enthusiastic voices of the congregation as they made their way to their seats. The Crawford and Harris families were greeted by the ushers at the front door and were shown to seats about mid-way up the aisle. Sarah sat at the end of the pew, next to the aisle.

Rainey Thompson saw them as they came in and was one of the first in the congregation to reach them in welcome. She gave Sarah a quick hug and waved down the pew as Sarah introduced her family.

As they stood for the first hymn, Sarah was startled as she felt a hand on her arm. She looked up and saw a pair of dark brown eyes and pleasant smile above a startlingly white dress shirt. "Is there room for one more?"

Sarah asked her family to scoot just a bit and nodded at Jared as she made room for him. It was tighter with Jared there than it had been, but he didn't seem to mind, nor did Sarah. Sarah's face warmed as their hands touched underneath the shared hymn book.

The service passed in a haze for Sarah. When it was time for the ushers to collect the offering, Jared stepped out to take his place at the front as the pastor prayed over this act of worship.

She was impressed by the message brought by the pastor, who preached about fear.

"Do we have more faith in our fear than we do in God? Do we find it easier to follow the loud voice of our fear, or to listen for the still, small voice of the Holy Spirit? God knows that we tend toward fear, but he constantly tells us to 'fear not.' Change is not our enemy – fear is," the pastor said.

During the invitation, Sarah bowed her head. As if he sensed her need for reassurance, Jared took her hand gently in his as the pastor prayed, only to let it go before anyone could see. She looked up at him with tears poised on her lashes, touched by his tenderness.

After the service, Jared was on hand to introduce them to different members of the congregation and the pastor, who told them that he hoped they would visit again real soon.

Jared introduced them to Tom, who had a handshake for each member of the family. The twins were completely mesmerized by the tall man when he tickled them under their chins. It didn't take much to bring forth a genuine giggle from either of the two girls.

A few of the younger female members of the congregation gave Sarah an appraising look, a smile on their faces that stopped before it got to their eyes – until those eyes rested on Jared. No doubt they couldn't help but notice the fact that Jared stayed by Sarah's side, his hand on her elbow and a flush on his face that looked slightly proprietary. Or was it her imagination?

One of the young women, Cynthia Baker, gave a brief greeting to Sarah and her family before she joined her friends down the aisle. For some reason, Sarah watched idly as she walked away. The glare that she had shot toward Jared surprised her. A few minutes later, they walked past the group, still deep in conversation, and she heard the words 'Jared' and 'Annabelle." Was one of these girls named Annabelle? Maybe he had a past with one of them. That thought made her frown slightly, but it disappeared when Jared took her elbow to escort her down the front steps of the church.

Before they parted, Mom reached out and touched Jared's arm gently. "Jared, won't you join us for lunch? Prudie put a couple of chickens in the oven before she left for church. I thought I'd make my famous potato salad to go with it, and we could eat out on the patio."

"I would love to, if it's not too much trouble." Jared looked at Sarah for approval.

Dad gave Mom a surprised look and then turned to Jared. "Good. You can follow us back to the house if you'd like. You're in for a treat."

"If you don't mind, I think I'll run home and change first, just in case." He touched Sarah's arm. "Would you like to run to my house with me and see a real-live beach house right on the water? We won't be another half-hour getting back to Pilot Oaks." Jared's eyes seemed almost to beg her to come with him.

"I'd love to . . . that is, if you and sis can take care of the potato salad?" Sarah looked at her mother's comical expression and laughed as she glanced up at the gentleman by her side.

"I think we can handle it," Susan said dryly. "I have to tell you something about my little sister, Jared. Martha Stewart, she isn't."

"I'm glad you came with me." Jared looked over at Sarah as he put the car in reverse. "I guess I wanted you to myself for just a little bit." He caught her looking at him with a slightly confused expression on her face.

She tilted her head, a slight frown on her brow, and a Mona Lisa half-smile on her lips. She hoped for an explanation of Jared's last statement.

"You are a man of surprises, Jared Benton. Today, especially. We hadn't talked about where you went to church. I guess I assumed you went to church somewhere, after our talk the other night on the beach. I, uh," Sarah stammered a bit and looked out the window to hide her blush. "I enjoyed sitting beside you in church." She stole a glance at him, relieved that he didn't laugh at her, but instead looked at her with a genuine expression on his face.

"As did I." He reached over and squeezed her hand as it sat in her lap.

They talked about the area they drove through as Jared pointed out this landmark and that. They shared bits of their past—but nothing of the future. Sarah didn't want to spoil the mood. The business? The inheritance? That could wait until later.

As they drove into the driveway of the beach house, Sarah couldn't help but be overwhelmed at the large modern structure. He led her inside, and from the entryway her eyes were immediately drawn across the room to a full wall of windows that faced the ocean. The modern sofas and chairs were tastefully arranged, the room not stark as many modern houses were, but a comfortable blend of angles and curves and warm colors. It was homey, if a house of this magnitude could be called homey.

"It's beautiful." She was in awe. "Did you pick everything out yourself?"

"Pretty much." He shrugged. "It's no house with rose bushes in front of it, but it's been a good house for me up until now."

"I would say so." Sarah turned to him, surprised at his lack of enthusiasm.

"Make yourself comfortable on the deck, if you'd like, while I go change. The view is spectacular." He winked as he slipped into real-estate mode.

WHEN SARAH and Jared drove up to Pilot Oaks and got out of the car, they could hear the welcome sounds of Abby's and Trudy's voices in the back yard with Oliver's barks interspersed between squeals.

Sarah looked down at her Sunday clothes and grimaced. "Now I feel grossly overdressed. Come on in, and I'll get changed before lunch."

He watched as she ran lightly up the stairs, as if she had been born here. He didn't want to eavesdrop, but when he heard his name, he couldn't help himself. He followed the scent of roasted chicken to the kitchen and peeked through the doorway.

Susan and Linda were working comfortably side-by-side as they peeled and chopped potatoes, onions, and pickles for what he presumed would be potato salad. Susan spoke. "Mom, what do you think about Sarah and Jared?"

Jared stood stock-still as he waited for Linda Crawford's answer.

She paused in slicing the potato in her hand. As she looked out the window for a second and then back at her eldest daughter, Jared heard her say, "I think Sarah's finally met someone who lives up to her dreams. You spent time with them together yesterday. What do you think?"

He felt the breath he had been involuntarily holding, release.

Susan chuckled at her mother's answer. "I'm with you. I told Sarah yesterday that every time he looked at her, you could tell that he was smitten with her. She blew it off, said she didn't want to think about it until the inheritance is decided. I think she's just a little scared at how fast things have moved. I like to tease, but I do want her to be happy."

"She knew about Marc's wedding, didn't she?" Linda's voice sounded worried, and Jared began to listen that much harder. Who was Marc?

"That's why she wanted to get here when she did. Would you believe Alice had the gall to send her an invitation?"

"I can't say I'm surprised. Sarah's done too good a job making everyone think she's perfectly fine. It's probably a good thing all this came up when it did."

Jared's brows creased. He knew the inheritance weighed heavily on Sarah. He had sensed that she felt responsible, for some reason, for the happiness and well-being of her family. Maybe because she was here first. Maybe because she was torn between a comfortable life at home in Kentucky and the unknown here in South Carolina. Maybe she was torn because there was someone back home that had a claim on her heart.

His attention was pulled back to the conversation in the kitchen when he heard Linda's soothing voice. "Anyway, that part of her life is over, and she would do well to move on."

"You don't think . . ."

"No, I don't think she still loves him, but he hurt her. She's probably a little wary of love right now."

Jared dipped his head. Who was this Marc, and what had he done to hurt Sarah? He felt anger well up in him for this unknown man who had apparently broken her heart.

Linda was still talking. "As for Jared, I know Sarah will be anxious to know where he stands in his walk with God. I think we have a little clearer picture there than we did, don't you? You know, Suze, I think he could be good for our Sarah."

Jared stepped through the doorway, and both women whirled around in surprise. Embarrassment stained their faces a bright crimson when they recognized him.

"I hope so." Jared spoke quietly as he calmed himself. He wanted to know about this Marc person, but he wanted more than anything to put these women, who were so important to Sarah, at ease. The last thing he wanted was for them to think he was angry. He quirked an eyebrow at them and smirked at the two matchmakers as he leaned back on the kitchen counter and crossed his arms in front of him.

"Now, if we can just convince Sarah of that fact." He arched an eyebrow and twisted his lips in concentration.

"I don't think it will be too difficult." Susan's expression was dry. "Just what are your intentions toward my little sister?"

Jared held up both hands in surrender as he laughed. "Purely honorable, I assure you!"

"What's going on?" Sarah walked into the kitchen to find Jared flanked by her mother and sister. All three of them laughed and had the grace to look just a little bit guilty.

AFTER LUNCH, before anything to do with business was mentioned, Robert raised his hand to speak. "We still need to pray some more, as a family, before we decide anything."

"That's a wise decision." Jared sat with the family out on the patio, elbows on his knees. "I've got a meeting at church at 5:00, and then the worship service after that. If you'd rather wait until in the morning to discuss it, that's fine, and if you want to go home and let me know later, that's fine, too."

Sarah shifted in her seat and stood. "I want to discuss it further, but I'd like to think some more first. I've got to take Oliver on a run. Anybody want to go with me?"

Jared looked up and caught her eye. "I'd like to go, if you don't mind." He handed her the leash that lay on the table next to him.

"Thank you, Jared." She was pleasant but stiff as she walked past him. When she put the leash on Oliver's collar, she started down the path immediately.

Robert looked after his youngest daughter in surprise and then shrugged his shoulders as Jared looked at him for guidance. "Maybe you can figure out what's eating her. She's been a little tense all day."

"I'll see what I can do." He looked at Robert intently. "I really do appreciate your stand. Alex never made any decisions without bathing it in prayer. It took me a while to appreciate it, but I've found that it's the only way to go, myself. Now, I'll see if I can catch her." Jared left them with a chuckle and a tilt to his head.

He jogged down the path to catch up with Sarah. When he reached out for her arm to stop her as he came up even with her, his smile faded. There were tears in her eyes. "Are you okay?"

Sarah hugged her arms to herself and looked away, tears pooling in her eyes. "I'm fine." Her tone was not convincing. "It's just a little much, you know?" She looked up into his eyes, and compassion welled up inside of him.

He rubbed the arm that he had reached out for when he stopped her and looked down for a minute. "What is?" He slid his hand down her arm and took her hand. His face grew tender as he looked at the slender fingers that he hoped someday to hear play the piano.

"The sermon today, the decision of whether to keep this house, the business . . . and everything. I know that God is bigger than our fears, but those fears are real. Sometimes, even though I know He's in control, He doesn't seem as real as those fears, you know?"

"I know. Alex talked to me about that several years ago. I was more or less raised in church, but the way we moved around, it never was important to my parents that we understand what we believed. Oh, Mom and Dad were

Christians. They were saved when they were younger, and they've since rededicated their lives and have become active in church. But when we were kids, Dad was always on the move, and Mom just tried to keep things going. They kind of lost sight of what was really important about faith. Before we lived here, we lived in military housing, and I hung out with just military kids. Military brats are tough, but it's because we're scared. I wanted to be tough more than anything, and it took me down some wrong roads. Alex was the one that pointed me in the right direction. He showed me that I couldn't let fear rule my life." Jared stopped and looked down again at the hand he held.

"I wish I had known him." Sarah spoke softly.

He tugged at her hand and led her down to the beach where Oliver could run. After Sarah stopped to take off her sandals, he kept her hand in his while they walked, talked, and let Ollie off the leash to chase waves. The breeze off the ocean, the water lapping at her toes, and the warmth of the summer sand started to work their magic.

"I wish you had, too. By the time he found out about all of you, he was too sick to act on it. He didn't want you to think that he wanted someone to take care of a sick old man."

His eyes misted as he told her of the last months of the old man's life. Even stricken with a terminal illness, he had come to the office, part of the day, every day that he possibly could.

"We spent a lot of time together those last months, and he taught me a lot about fear and about grace. He taught me not to be afraid to take a chance when it came to trust in God. When I finally learned to do that, I listened more. God had talked to me all along – I-+ hadn't stopped long enough to hear Him."

Sarah listened quietly, and he tried to read the expression on her face. Did she understand what he was trying to explain?

"Sarah." He tipped her chin up with his finger so he could look into her eyes. "When I saw you on the boardwalk . . ."

Her eyes latched on to his. "Why haven't you said anything about it? At first I thought you didn't remember."

"Oh, I remember. I'll never forget it."

"Then why . . .?"

"I don't know. Guilt, I guess. Alex had told me what he found out about all of you. He even showed me your picture." He shrugged and looked away for a moment. "I wanted to see you before we met. I guess I wanted to get an idea of what kinds of people were coming to take away what I had worked for." He couldn't meet her eyes.

"Jared."

He looked up and saw the gentle look on her face.

"I probably would have done the same thing." She laughed on a leftover sob. "You didn't count on meeting Oliver first."

"No." He gazed at her and then sighed. "To be honest, I didn't want to like you. I wanted to be angry."

"But you're not."

"No."

His brows furrowed as he rubbed the insides of her wrists, and then he gazed into her hazel eyes. He swallowed in an effort to keep emotion out of his voice. "I don't want you to make any decision based on fear, or on what the money would do for you, or on what you think the others in your family want you to do. I'll leave soon. You all need to pray about it, and then talk about it. You decide what's best for you. You'll get your answer. I'm praying for you, too, you know." He grinned at her as he shook his head, almost in disbelief at the jumble of feelings coursing through him.

"Thank you."

"Not a problem." A smile hovered on his lips. "I know you'll get your answer. I trust God to give you the one that will make you happy."

But did that answer include him?

CHAPTER FIFTEEN

*H*e left her on the beach, very tempted to call someone to say he couldn't make the committee meeting. But he knew she needed time to think and pray. She had made him promise to come back after church. He could tell that she wanted to reach some kind of decision, even if it was a decision to wait.

As he traveled to the church building, he thought about the afternoon he'd spent with the Crawford family. They were easy to be with, very warm and friendly, and they watched him closely. They didn't give their trust easily, but he sensed that they would be gracious to a fault until they found reason not to trust him. He hoped that he had passed the test.

His thoughts wandered to the meeting he was about to attend – it was that time of year again. The Budget Committee was up to their ears in budget revisions and requests. On top of the usual revisions in preparation for a new church year, the search committee had put together a salary package for a new staff member. So far, there hadn't been any dissension in the group, but tonight might be a different story. A new committee member started tonight. Cynthia Baker.

Jared sighed. For the last ten years, if he said something was white, Cynthia found a way to be on hand to say it was black.

He would have stayed on the beach with Sarah until dark if she'd asked, but she, as well as he, knew that their family needed this time without an outsider to make the decisions that needed to be made. And his church needed him. He could thank Alex for that, too.

Jared pursed his lips thoughtfully when he considered that first paycheck he got from Alex when he joined him in the real estate firm. He looked it over and talked about all the things he wanted to do with it. Alex came up and looked over his shoulder.

"Boy, you know what I'd do if I were you?" Alex narrowed his eyes and looked closely at the young man.

Jared smirked at him. He knew pretty much what he was about to say. "And what's that, Mr. Crawford?"

"I'd sit down before I ever went to the bank and figure up where-all it's goin'. Ten percent to the church – always off the top, I figure; ten percent to the savings account, and then the rest you live on. Feel free to enhance any of those figures," he said, then winked at Jared and walked out the door.

Alex had been good to him. He started a life of stewardship that day. He took the tithe—ten percent—off the top, put aside money for the future, and then spent wisely the balance. As a result, he had, at thirty, what he would have considered at one time a fortune. He thought about the family that was, right now, perhaps in prayer about their part in the business that he had helped build with their unknown relative. He had a feeling Alex would have loved them, too.

Now if he could convince Cynthia to be a productive part of this committee, his day would have been made. Jared conjured up an image of Sarah waving at him from the beach. That should hold him until after the meeting.

SARAH WALKED BACK to the house with Oliver after spending the better part of the hour since Jared left in prayer—and this time she listened as well as talked. She felt fairly confident for her part. She didn't quite know how to tell her family what she had decided. She had prayed about that part, too.

She entered the house from the back around 7:00. It was quiet. The girls were likely asleep in their portable crib upstairs. Her parents, sister, and brother-in-law were sitting and talking quietly in the less-formal parlor.

"Hey everybody." Sarah entered the room quietly. "I'm sorry for the way I ran out of here earlier."

"Come and sit between us." Mom patted the couch where she and Dad sat together. "I was about ready to send out a search party. We thought we should pray together before we make any decisions or even talk about it anymore."

Dad took her hand and looked at her with love. "You didn't do anything wrong, in my eyes. You were upset and you needed to get away to think about it. We understand that. Lots going on these days, huh?"

Fresh tears threatened as she looked at her father and then at her mother. She nodded. "I love you, you know." She smiled as she hugged them through her tears.

"Let's pray before we talk. Sound good?" Dad looked around at his family gathered there together. They each reached their hands out and formed a circle of love and faith that would stand the test of time, of misunderstandings, and of distance. Each of them prayed; they shared their hearts with God and with one another through that prayer.

They asked for guidance as they made decisions that would affect them all. They prayed for one another and for Jared, who had been kind to them when they were strangers. They sat, heads bowed and eyes closed, in silence to give them the opportunity to listen for a word from God. When they raised their heads, there was not a dry eye in the room.

Dad spoke. "I need you all to tell me what you think is the answer that God has given you—not us—you, about the business and the house. I just get the feeling that we don't have to agree on this to be able to do what God wants us to do. Whatever we decide, we've been blessed beyond measure. God's grace is good."

"God is good, all the time." Sarah nodded and thought of Jared. He had said that the night they went out on a date together and ended up on the beach with Ollie.

"That He is." Dad smiled at her. "Why don't we start with you, Sarah? You've had the inside track, since you've been here longer."

"If you don't care, Dad, I'd rather hear what all of you have to say first. I know what my answer is, and I think I'll be able to tell you better when I know what you want to do." Sarah felt calmer than she had two days ago. She waved her hand when she saw the worried look on the faces of her family and teased them just a little. "Don't worry; I won't change my answer to fit yours."

"Well, all right, we'll go first." Susan looked at Mike, who nodded at her to continue. "We looked at the financial picture. We know that this is a good business. It has steadily made money even in recession. The house is a dream come true. We're not ready to make a move to South Carolina, but, since Mike and I do have a rudimentary understanding of business, we would like to retain my portion of the business as a partner. We may eventually want to move here, but for now, we'll stay in Kentucky and look upon this as an investment in our future."

"What about the house?" Sarah was curious that she hadn't mentioned it except in passing.

"I'm not sure. I've got some ideas, but I'd like to hear the rest of your comments on that before I share."

"Okay, the Harris contingent being heard from, we'll go next." Dad looked beyond Sarah to catch his wife's nod of encouragement. "We would like to retain our part of the business, too. It would make retirement a lot easier and help us to be able to travel more, even if it's just to South Carolina. I'm like Susan. I'm not sure we're ready to move down here full-time, but your mother and I have a little proposal about the house – after we've heard from Sarah."

Sarah's confidence grew with each of her family members' answers to the questions surrounding the inheritance. It seemed that they all had different ideas about the inheritance, but similar goals. She squeezed her father's hand and looked around at each of her loved ones as she began.

"I have been so worried about this. I don't know why. I told Jared earlier that I had let myself get distracted by many things. On the way down here, I made a promise to God, that I would take the opportunity to listen to Him and to follow His lead in decisions about my future. It's almost as if as soon as I learned about the extent of this inheritance, I turned that part of me off. I was afraid. I was afraid of making wrong decisions; I was torn between what I wanted and what I thought you would want me to do. The sermon this morning hit me between the eyes, which is why I was a little crazy today." She looked down at her hands, which were clasped in her lap.

"I've decided that the best thing for me, and what I want, right now, is to move to South Carolina." She paused and then got up the nerve to look up at them. She had almost let fear creep back in. The last thing she wanted was to disappoint them. To her surprise, each of her family members simply sat and studied her expectantly. At their looks of love and acceptance, the tears came back, but this time they were tears of relief.

Mom put her arms around Sarah. Tears were in her eyes, too. "Sweetheart, we knew you were unhappy in your job and in other things. You tried it. You moved back to your home town, but it wasn't the same, was it? Even in your own house?"

She didn't want her mother to think she was miserable. "I wasn't completely unhappy. It was more that I knew there was something else out there, you know? I didn't want to think I'd wasted my education. Putting me through school wasn't easy for you guys. But then after Marc..."

Her mom took her hand. "Oh, sweetie . . ."

"No, it's okay. After Marc and I broke up, I knew I'd let things slide. I had drifted into a relationship I thought was a good, safe bet. I was ready to settle down. But you know what?" Sarah stopped and almost laughed. "God wasn't ready for me to settle down. He was ready for me to depend on Him."

Mom gave her a quick hug. "And now you have the opportunity to try new things. We're called to do many things in our lives, and your music isn't what you do, it's who you are. Who knows? Maybe God has called you, now, to be an example for us? When your dad, Susan, and Mike saw how you enjoyed being around the office yesterday, we 'put out the fleece' so to speak, and the answer to our prayers is what we thought it might be."

Sarah knew, then, that her mother didn't want to tell her what to do, but wanted, instead, for her to do what God told her to do. She saw a peace in her mother's eyes.

Sarah looked around at her family. She wanted to remember this moment. "I love this house. I know I saw it for the first time this week, but I think it will be significant to us, somehow. I don't know that I would want to live in it full-time like Uncle Alex, but I want to keep it. Jared said he had always told him that it would make a fantastic bed-and-breakfast, with the marsh and ocean views and enough land to make it feel like you're out in the country. I don't know. What do you think?" She looked nervously from face to face. Sarah hadn't voiced this idea to anyone, but when Jared had mentioned it to her that first day, the idea had taken root, and every time she looked at the bedrooms, she couldn't help but think of the happy families and couples that might stay there in the future.

Susan and her mother looked at one another and laughed out loud. "Well, the fleece has come back, and like in Gideon's day of old, the fleece is wet, and the ground all around it is dry," Mom said.

Dad looked around at his family a little pensively. No doubt this was new territory for them. God had answered this prayer, but there would be so many more prayers offered up. They couldn't stop, now.

"God has blessed us, family. Sarah, your mother and I have prayed about what our part in this inheritance would be. This is a grand old house." His gaze traveled around at the room and then settled back on his family. "I'm like you, Sarah, I can't imagine this as a home, but I think it would be great to be able to share it with people who need to get away from the cares of everyday life. I like the idea of a bed-and-breakfast operation."

Mom held up her hand for their attention. "Your father and I have talked, and we would like to move here about half the year – tourist season – for a few years and try to run this as a bed and breakfast. Eventually, we might want to live here full-time, but for now, we'd like to do it on a trial basis, see what God has for us. What do you think, girls?"

"I think it's a great idea." Mike beat the two girls to the punch. "I would love to be a part of that. I can help you with the legalities and financials of the operation. Susan and I talked about what a great business that would be in this area, and if the time came that, as a family, we no longer wanted to operate it as such, but wanted it to be a family home, it wouldn't be a problem."

"So, we're agreed?" Sarah looked at each of her family members in wonder. She praised God in her heart that each of them had a different take on the inheritance, but each wanted to be a part of it. They would work through all this together. Her heart seemed to skip a beat when she looked at her watch, which read 8:30.

"I asked Jared to stop by after church." There was a slight flush on her cheeks at the mention of his name. "We can tell him what we've decided and then call Mr. Schumaker in the morning." She felt joy bubbling up in her as she turned and hugged her father impulsively. "He's such a nice man, Dad. You'll really like him. His daughter is expecting twins, too. And they're his first grandchildren."

"Sounds like I already have something in common with him." Dad hugged Sarah. He patted her on the shoulder with a mixture of sadness and pride in his eyes.

It hit her just a little. She would be leaving home.

All thoughts of sadness left her when she heard the doorbell ring. She jumped up and sprinted to the front door, her face flushed with relief and excitement. She expected Jared. What she did not expect was the slight jolt when her eyes met the sparkling brown eyes of the man in her dreams.

JARED FOUND himself seated next to Sarah on the settee as they gathered in the library to discuss what had been decided. Robert took the lead, as head of the family and seemed pleased that Jared seemed receptive to their plans for the house.

"I've always thought this would be a great bed and breakfast, and I told Alex as much." He grinned. "Thing was, he liked to live where he could smell the marsh and hear the waves crash. It's more house than I would ever want, but then Sarah knows what my tastes run to."

Jared looked at Sarah, and she felt the heat rise in her cheeks. She thought of the difference between the modern beach-house and the frame house down the road, pretty sure about which house he preferred. She didn't blame him. One was a house, the other had been, and still was, a home.

"Would you like me to set up an appointment with another bed and breakfast owner in the area? Maybe in Charleston or Myrtle Beach? I know several, and those areas wouldn't be so much competition as a support system." Jared chuckled and shook his head in disbelief. "I got so excited about the house that I forgot to ask you about the business."

Sarah suddenly found her hands very interesting as she paused. Suddenly, she felt unsure. He had indicated he wouldn't mind being in a partnership with them, but did he, deep down, want to have complete control of the business? Would this affect what she perceived as a possible relationship between the two of them?

"We've decided that, at least for now, we would like to retain our partnerships in the real estate business. Mom and Dad, and Mike and Susan will be more like 'silent partners,' but . . ."

"But?"

"But, I plan to move down here, and I'd really like to work in the business, if you think I could do it." She shifted her glance back down to clasped hands, her knuckles white.

"Are you kidding?" The relief in his voice was obvious. "I think you'll be a great asset to our company." He reached unconsciously for her hand, which she gave readily. He looked into her eyes and nodded his head as he smiled. He startled when he heard a throat clear, having forgotten for a moment that Sarah's family was there in the room with them.

Robert chuckled. "Sarah, the first time I talked to Jared on the phone, he told me the same thing—that you'd be a natural at real estate, but basically you were more concerned about us than you were about what you wanted. He didn't say that in so many words, but since we've been down here, I've seen the same thing."

Linda nodded her head in agreement. "Sarah, you're a big

girl. You've thought about everyone but you for much too long, and it's time that you started to consider what you want out of life. I can already see that you're happier here than at home." A look passed between mother and daughter that hinted at a hidden meaning. Was Linda referring to Marc? Sarah opened her mouth to say something, but Linda held up her hand to stop her. "This came at just the right time, didn't it? God's timing is always better than ours, you know." Sarah's mother laughed a little as she grabbed a tissue from the box on the coffee table. "Okay, before anybody starts patting me on the shoulder, I'm not crying because my baby's decided to move away. I'm crying because I love it when God puts a plan together. And He did."

"I guess the next major hurdle will be to tell Lucy. She won't be happy, I can tell you." Sarah cringed at the thought of the scene that Lucy was fully capable of when she found out Sarah had decided to move to South Carolina instead of remaining at their school.

"Lucy will be fine. You can't run your life to please your friends any more than you can run your life to please your family – although if I were to choose, I'd choose us any day." Susan laughed at her own joke, even as she wiped the mist from her eyes. Mike slipped an arm around his wife's waist and pulled her close to him.

Sarah chuckled as she nodded agreement with her sister. "I guess I need to call her and tell her. I'll have to go home and get my stuff, and then decide where to live in the meantime. I don't think I want to rattle around this big house by myself and I don't know that Prudie wants to baby sit me full-time. Don't suppose you know of a good real estate firm?" Sarah looked at Jared with a glint in her eye.

"Just might be able to help you. Do you plan to stay a little bit longer after your folks leave, or do you want to fly back with them?" Jared had already thought of several condos and houses that were available—in his neighborhood.

"I guess if I'm moving down here, I should stay a few more days and find a place to live, and then drive back for my things. I'll have to get my house in Summerville ready to sell, so I'll want my car there." She exhaled as though she had been holding her breath. Her expression, though, held a hint of excitement. She looked at Jared, eyes wide, and flushed when he winked at her.

"Wow," she said. "This is really happening."

CHAPTER SIXTEEN

"*L*uce, it's Sarah. I need to talk to you as soon as possible – it's important. Call me back?" Sarah sighed as she looked down at Oliver. "She didn't pick up. I hope she doesn't wait too long to call." She grimaced a little. "I've got my nerve up now." She gave Ollie a good rub and fetched his leash to take him down to the beach for a run before bedtime.

She stood in the hallway and peered into the library where her family and Jared still sat. Pausing a few minutes, she relaxed a little as she listened to the excited chatter coming from the room. Jared's eye's met hers, his eyebrows raised in response. She held up the leash, and he gave her a quick nod and a brilliant smile. At this, Mom glanced in the direction he had looked to see Sarah caught in the maze of that smile.

Suddenly, Mom rose from her seat. "Can I interest any of you in some leftover dessert?" She chuckled when she spied the boyish look on Jared's face. "Don't worry. We'll save some for you and Sarah."

"Thanks." He squeezed her hand, and then he raced to the hallway to meet Sarah and Oliver.

"DID YOU GET YOUR FRIEND?" They walked side-by-side. Oliver ran in and out of the waves on the darkening beach. He had found pieces of seaweed and the occasional driftwood to worry and left his mistress and Jared alone for a moment, or until he found something that he couldn't resist bringing up to show them.

"Lucy didn't answer." There was a worried tone in her voice. "Lucy and I have been friends since high school. We've been pretty much inseparable. We didn't room together in college, but we may as well have. She's constantly tried to fix me up with this or that eligible bachelor." Sarah laughed as she told him about some of the blind dates she had endured at Lucy's hands.

Jared laughed with her. "I guess everybody has a friend like that. Tom would be mine. Thank goodness guys don't get off on matchmaking quite like girls do. At least I don't think they do."

"Hey, maybe we should just set Tom and Lucy up, and get them off *our* backs!" Sarah laughed. When she looked over at him, her eyes widened with surprise at the speculative gleam in his eye. "You're not serious? You're as much a matchmaker as Lucy!" She gave him a swat on the arm, and he dodged her, and then grabbed her around the waist to protect himself as they both laughed.

When he pulled her toward him, he felt her quick intake of breath. "I'm glad you've decided not to leave here for good." He still held on to her as she met his gaze with almost wonder in her eyes. He let her go, but then took her hand and tugged her along to walk beside him. She didn't have much to say after that, but stole glances at him every so often.

What were you thinking? Great job, Benton. You need to slow down, or you'll scare her off, he thought. She's a business partner. If you grab her every time you think about it, you'll sure have the rumor-mill in full force quickly—because if you're completely honest with yourself, you know you want to grab her, and often. He was glad it was almost dark. It helped to hide the redness he felt creeping up to his neck and cheeks.

TRUE TO HIS WORD, Jared took Sarah and her mom to look at some condos and houses the next morning. "I thought your mom might want to come with you to see some places before she left."

"That was very thoughtful of you." Sarah was surprised, but then again, not. Last night had changed the dynamic between them somewhat. She felt shyer around him now than when she had first met him. What she had seen in his eyes the night before was what she had seen in the eyes of the man in her dream. It was what she had been looking for with Marc, but never quite found.

When they walked into the third property, a little house right on the beach in Murrells Inlet, Sarah knew that she had come home. From the front door, she could see straight through the living and dining areas to the beach beyond.

"This is the one." Sarah had looked in all the nooks and crannies of the two-bedroom, two-bath cottage. "Do you think I can get it?" Her mom had already voiced her approval and had left them to look more closely at the kitchen and laundry areas.

"I don't think it will be a problem – you already own twenty percent of it." He grinned. "The company owns it as a rental right now. I thought you might want to 'try before you buy,' and this one is available."

"That's a good idea." She was suddenly nervous. "There's a lot to think about, isn't there?"

JARED WATCHED as her emotions changed from delight to uncertainty and an emotion he couldn't pinpoint. Maybe doubt? One thing was sure: she had fallen in love with the beach house at first sight. He didn't want to see her revert to worry.

Jared leaned against the doorway between the living and dining rooms. He thought about taking her hand, caressing her fingers, taking her into his arms—anything to reassure her, but then he pulled back. He would use a subtler approach. One step at a time. She had decided to move here. A week ago, he hadn't met her and was suspicious of a family from Kentucky that was going to bilk him out of sixty percent of the business he helped build. Now he couldn't imagine life without her. Now he had to pull himself back into the conversation before she began to think he had lost his mind. Sarah wasn't the only one having trouble adjusting.

He stood up a little straighter. "Hey, all these decisions don't have to be made at once, you know. Take it one step at a time. Let's get things started on this place and get your folks taken to the airport today, and then tomorrow, you can come out to the office, we'll introduce you around, and let everybody know you're here to stay." His countenance brightened at the thought.

"Thank you." Sarah took a deep breath. "I don't know why you've done so much for me and for my family, but I appreciate it. Maybe after I find my way around, you won't think of me as an albatross hung around your neck." She laughed a little nervously and glanced away.

"Oh, I don't look at you like that at all." His voice was soft as he answered. He hadn't missed the shift in her face from relaxed confidence to a feminine awareness of him that he had noticed when they got too close. When she looked back at him, he put his hands in his pockets and shrugged.

When her mom came back into the room, Sarah had schooled her features, but Jared saw that the blush was still there. Would Sarah's mother feel uncomfortable leaving her baby girl here, among strangers in a strange land? Did she see him as a stranger? Or did she already see him as someone who might just be falling in love with her daughter? He had to smile when Linda Crawford, as they left the house, grinned at him with amusement and winked.

SARAH WAS quiet on the drive back to Pilot Oaks after they watched the Cessna with her family onboard take off from Charleston, headed for Nashville. She leaned back on the headrest and looked over at Jared. He had a contented look on his face as he drove, and he didn't seem to mind the quiet. It allowed her some time to think and reflect on the last few days. She saw a smile flit across his lips and wondered what he was thinking. There was no way she could get up the nerve to ask him. When she recalled their walk on the beach the evening before, her face warmed, and she had to look out the window. What would he think if he looked at her just now?

The ring of her cell phone broke into the quiet, and when she answered it, she squealed. "Lucy! Where have you been?" She jumped in her seat in excitement. Jared chuckled and nodded his head.

"Sorry, Sarah, my phone's been on the fritz for a week, and I just got a new one today. I was afraid I would have umpteen billion messages by now, but I didn't – just ten billion from you."

Sarah laughed and then sighed. She could feel herself relax.

"Oh, Luce. There's so much I've got to tell you. I don't know if I can even begin to tell you over the phone . . ."

"Well, before you start, have you met any eligible bachelors down there?"

Sarah looked over at Jared, who gave her a quizzical look. Sarah laughed and thought, if he only knew.

"Actually, Luce, I have." She spoke cryptically, so Jared wouldn't know the context of the answer. "And I might actually have one for you when you come down to visit."

At that statement, Jared looked at her with an eyebrow cocked. Sarah simply twisted her lips and looked at him appraisingly as she continued the conversation with her friend.

She almost forgot that she wasn't alone in the car. There was so much to tell. She told Lucy about her first encounter with Mr. Schumaker, the tour of Pilot Oaks, the real estate business. Everything that did not include personal information about Jared Benton.

"Mom, Dad, Susan, Mike, and the girls will be home tonight, if you want to pick their brains a bit, and I'll be home this weekend." Sarah paused a minute before she broached the next topic. "Lucy, there is one thing I didn't tell you, and you might not like it."

"What is it?" Lucy asked, her tone curious.

"Well . . . I guess there's only one way to say it, and that's to say it straight out . . . I'm moving to South Carolina." Sarah said it quietly as she glanced over at Jared for moral support.

"Shut up!" Lucy instantly resorted to high school vernacular, translated loosely, "no way!"

Sarah laughed. When Lucy responded like this, it was with more excitement than anger. She felt like she'd dodged a bullet on this one.

"Are you serious? Okay, I've got to meet this eligible bachelor of yours – you said you might have one for me, too? When do you move . . . I'll come down with you to help you bring your stuff and get settled in . . . wait – this means you won't come back to school this fall . . ." In musical terms, Lucy's voice had gone from an excited fortissimo into a decrescendo and on to a pianissimo in the space of about ten seconds.

"Yeah, Luce. That's what it means." Sarah looked out the window with a sad little smile on her face as she blinked back a stray tear. "We inherited a real estate business, and I want to give it a try. I've always got my teaching certificate if it doesn't work out, but, Luce, I really hope it will."

"Wow. I didn't see this coming. I guess I knew we'd be separated eventually . . . I mean, best friends can't stay joined at the hip forever if they want any kind of life, now can they . . . but I sure will miss you. On the other hand, now I'll have a place to go on vacation!"

Lucy could talk herself into and out of a depression quicker than anyone Sarah had ever seen. That was one of the things that endeared Lucy to her. She could be down in the dumps with you, and at the same time, pull you up to see every positive aspect of any situation.

"I was thinking about what you said . . . yeah, why don't you help me move? School won't start until the first of August, and I've already got a place picked out, so I won't have to wait until I sell my house to move. That might give you a couple of weeks in July to come with me and see the sights. Who knows, maybe you'll fall in love with the place as well." Sarah looked over at Jared, and then blushed when she realized what she had just said.

She ended the conversation about the time they arrived back at Pilot Oaks and brushed a tear from her cheek. She knew Jared saw, but he didn't say anything. He simply got out of the car and went around to open her door for her. He squeezed her hand as he took it to help her out of the SUV. "Tough conversation?"

"Not really." She realized, then, that it hadn't been as hard as she thought it would be. "I miss Lucy more than I realized. I guess we have to grow up sometime, don't we? If not, I'd be high-tailing it back to Kentucky with my family."

"I'm anxious to meet this Lucy. When I saw how little you

had to do to keep the conversation afloat, I assumed that she must be the life of the party."

"You have no idea." Sarah laughed with him as they walked up the path to the front porch.

CHAPTER SEVENTEEN

On Tuesday morning, Sarah and Prudie worked side-by-side in the bright, cheery kitchen. The white subway tile with green accents sparkled in the sunshine streaming through the over-sized windows in the completely modernized kitchen – modernized, but with historical touches that made the kitchen fit into the historical period of the house.

Sarah wasn't used to servants that waited on her, and Prudie seemed to appreciate the way Sarah treated her, as if she were simply a good friend and respected member of the family.

They sat together at the kitchen table. It was the first day Sarah was to report to the office. When she didn't say anything for a few minutes, Prudie reached over to squeeze her hand.

"You'll be fine, Sarah. What are you nervous about?" The sympathy and care in Prudie's eyes encouraged her to face her fears.

"I don't really know." A confused little laugh escaped her. "All of the sudden, I realize how little I really know about this business. I don't even know whether I'll be any good at it." That niggling fear had grown by leaps and bounds.

Prudie just laughed. "That reminds me of a young man that

once said basically the same thing to me. He had graduated from college with honors—a pre-law degree, no less—and after a bit of upheaval in his life decided that instead of law school, he would go into the real estate business. He had an experienced partner who had mentored him and had implicit faith in him, but when it came down to taking responsibility for his decision, he felt like he was in over his head."

"What did he do?" Sarah asked the question quietly. She had a feeling she knew of whom Prudie spoke.

"He swallowed that last bit of fear and went for it. He knew that if it didn't work out, he could always go to law school. Just like you. If this isn't something you want to do, you have your teaching degree and your musical ability. One decision does not a lifetime make, you know." Prudie looked deeply into Sarah's eyes. "Have you prayed about this?"

"Yes. Over and over again." Sarah wanted to feel better, felt guilty because she didn't feel better, but she didn't.

"Well, stop praying and start trusting. If you feel like you've had an answer, then act on that answer, and stop waiting for the revised version." She had a look on her face that lightened what might have been a harsh statement.

Sarah smiled back at Prudie. She got up from the table and gave Prudie a hug. "Thanks, Prudie. I'll be okay. It's just kind of 'first-day jitters,' I guess. God didn't bring me down here to drop me now, did He?"

"That He did not. He's got a plan for you here. I just have a feeling. He has a plan for all of us, and I think all of us fit into that plan together, somehow."

"The young man was Jared, wasn't it?" Sarah gazed at the dear one who in the space of five short days had come to mean so much to her.

"Yes, it was. Alex talked him into partnering with him instead of going to law school. I think in a way he's regretted that he didn't finish his course, but he loved real estate too much to pass up the opportunity when Alex offered it. And, I think he just wanted to stick closer to home at that time in his life. I'm sure he'll tell you about it someday."

Sarah wondered at Prudie's words. What had happened that made Jared turn completely from his career path? She felt some peace as Prudie's words and confidence sank in, and on the very heels of the wave of peace her eyes widened, and she gasped when she saw the clock on the wall, next to the sink. "Oh no! I've got to get going. I can't be late today of all days! What would everyone think?"

"They'd probably think that this young lady has had a lot of decisions to make over the last few days, and that a little extra sleep might not be such a bad thing for her." Prudie's words calmed her, and her lips twisted in a smile as she tilted her head and put her hand on Sarah's arm. "You'll be okay. You probably won't even be late."

"Thanks, Prudie. I'm glad you're here. Are you sure Ollie won't be too much trouble for you?" Sarah still felt anxious, as if any excuse to avoid the day would do.

"No, we'll get along fine, won't we, fella?" Prudie looked down at the dog who had found himself a place next to the back door. Prudie had put his dog bed and toys there, and now that was "his spot." "You go on, and don't give us another thought."

"Okay. I'm going. Thanks again, and I'll see you tonight." Sarah kissed Prudie on the cheek and gathered up her purse and planner as she headed toward the door.

"I'll be praying for you." Prudie called out just as Sarah was about to close the door.

Sarah couldn't be sure, but she thought she heard her say, ". . . for both of you."

As SARAH PULLED into the lot outside the office, she felt her knees tremble and her hands shake just a little as she put the car in park. "Okay, Lord, I'm here, where I think you want me to be. My hands are off, and I ask you—no, I beg you—to remind me that I've done that. I know I don't have to ask you to put your hands on, because they never came off, did they?" Sarah straightened her spine and took a deep breath. "Thank you, Lord. I know you're with me today, and that you are good—all the time."

She gathered her things, locked her car, and walked in the front door of the office. The smiling face of the receptionist greeted her immediately.

"Good morning, Miss Weaver." Sarah spoke to the young lady at the desk, who had risen at her entrance.

"Please, call me Carla." Her voice was warm and welcoming. "Mr. Benton asked me show you right to his office as soon as you came in. Would you like some coffee? I just made a fresh pot."

"That would be great! I'm a firm believer that the morning doesn't get a good start until the second cup of coffee." Sarah liked Carla. "How long have you worked here?"

"I've been here about two years. I went to school and got an associate's degree in Office Management, and I guess you could say this has been my first 'real' job." She sent a genuine smile Sarah's way. "I like working here. Mr. Crawford was a sweetheart, and Mr. Benton is great to work for." Carla led Sarah to Jared's private office.

"Coffee, Mr. Benton? We have a fresh pot." Carla came in with Sarah. Jared looked up from his desk at Carla's voice and saw Sarah. His smile, which he would have had for anyone that came to his door, deepened and reached his eyes when he saw her.

"Thanks. I could use another cup. Sarah?"

"Already put in my order, thanks. Carla's taken good care of me from the front door to here." Sarah grinned at the girl and tilted her head as she looked at Jared.

"Coffee coming right up, then—cream or sugar?" When Jared shook his head "no," and Sarah said "two sugars," she nodded and made her exit.

"Thanks, Carla," Sarah called after her.

"You have a great staff, from what I've seen so far." Sarah didn't seem to know what to do with her hands. She was a little nervous now that they were alone.

"*We* have a great staff, Sarah. Remember that." He smirked at the flush that came over her face when he reminded her that she wasn't just a visitor anymore.

"I know. It won't be easy to switch to management mode, especially when they all know way more about the business than I probably ever will know." As she said that, she suddenly felt at a loss.

"I thought about that this morning. I know you want to go back to Kentucky this weekend, and we'll need to get things set up for the house for when you get back. How about we get the house affairs settled today, and I'll show you some of the projects I've kept my hand in?"

"That sounds fine. I'll follow your lead." Sarah was relieved that he had thought about her role, since she didn't have a clue what it would be. When Carla came back in and handed her a cup of coffee, she mouthed a quiet "thanks."

"You're welcome. Let me know if you need anything, okay?"

Jared looked up. "Thanks, Carla." He continued with Sarah. "I think once you get the feel for the area, you will be really valuable as we scout out new properties. We still do quite a few flips. We just do them as a corporate business now instead of like when I was in college. Some folks make their living with flips, but I like more variety than that. Some of the flips we do, we keep for vacation rentals if they're in a good location, and some we have open houses and sell off."

"That sounds interesting." Sarah leaned forward a little in the chair across from Jared's desk.

Sarah felt the adrenaline rush at the prospects before her. In this business, there would be variety, a different kind than she'd ever known as a student or even as a teacher. It enticed her and excited her.

Jared nodded. "I don't want to mislead you. It can be a lot of hard work, but it can be fun, too. When I think about that first flip that Tom and I did . . . Wow. We stripped the insides of that place out, ourselves, and did most of the reconstruction, too. Now we have contractors that work for us, but sometimes, in a crunch, we have to get our hands dirty."

"Does Tom keep his hand in real estate?" Sarah thought of Jared and Tom as poor college students making their mark on the real estate world one house at a time.

"Naw, he's too busy with what he calls his 'real job.'" Jared laughed. His regard for his friend and his occupation shone through even as he teased. "For some reason, he thinks that detective work is more meaningful that fixing up houses to sell."

"I guess we all have our calling." Sarah grinned at the boyish expression on his face.

"Yeah, Tom decided that real estate was not his calling on the last flip we did where he had to dig up a septic tank. Not a pretty job. When we finished that one, he applied to the police academy!" Jared laughed.

"But it didn't faze you?" Sarah asked, wondering what the difference was. After her conversation with Prudie, she was curious to know why he had given up dreams of a law career to fix up and sell houses.

He shrugged. "Not really. I've gotten into some pretty bad situations, but I always looked on it as a challenge, you know? I always did like to finish a project, and that's what real estate is – one project after another."

"I think I know what you mean." She knew she would like to explore this train of thought later.

"Let's take you around the office again. There are a few key people that you need to get to know really well." He rose from his chair and came around to the door.

As he opened it, he touched her arm and gestured for her to precede him into the hallway. She felt the blush rise on her cheek, and when she looked up at him, she noticed a tinge of red gracing the tips of his ears as well. Interesting.

The head sales agent was Ben Lockhart. When they entered his office, Sarah took note of the various fishing paraphernalia, mounted fish, and trophies that lined his walls and book cases. A photo of a family looked up at her from the credenza behind his desk, introduced to her as himself, his wife Lily, and two sons. Sarah had met Ben briefly the week before, with the other staff. In his late thirties, his reddish hair was echoed in the photo of his two boys.

"Hey, Ben. You remember Sarah?"

"Sure! Nice to see you again!" Ben stood and shook her hand warmly.

Jared stuck his hands in his pockets. "It looks like she's going to be a part of our little family."

"Great! We can use some extra hands around here – especially with the big open house day we've got coming up this fall!" Ben had risen from his seat to shake Sarah's hand and motioned for her to sit.

"No. We can't stop right now. I just wanted you to know that in a few weeks, she'll be here with us full-time. She'll be assisting me some and will have some projects of her own, but I want her to learn about all aspects of the business. You know we'll all be on hand for the big day." Jared waved at Ben as he held out his hand to Sarah to direct her into the hallway. "She'll be in to see you once she gets back to stay."

"Good to see you, Ben. I'm sure I'll learn a lot from you!" She turned and waved at the still-standing man.

"Hey, when you get settled in, I'll be sure that Maggie gives you a call. We'll have you out for a barbecue." He winked at her and waved as the two left his office.

Out in the hallway, Jared leaned over to Sarah and waggled his eyebrows. "Ben barbecues the best ribs in the county. When he invites you, be sure to ask if you can bring a date . . . and then ask me!"

Sarah laughed. The idea that Jared, the boss, had to finagle his way into an invitation to a barbecue was ridiculous but endearing.

CHAPTER EIGHTEEN

$\mathcal{S}$arah and Oliver left for Kentucky on Thursday morning after spending two days absorbing as much of the Crawford and Benton atmosphere as possible. Jared noticed that the more she learned about the business, the more questions she asked. That was a good sign.

She hadn't even been gone two days, and he already missed her. He still hadn't admitted to himself, fully, why he felt this way, and he was in no hurry to analyze why he felt so good in her presence. His biggest fear, right now, was that she would get back home and decide that she couldn't bear to leave.

Why would she consider a relationship with him? She didn't really know him. She saw what he was now—the successful businessman—but what about what he had been in the past? Sometimes the past loomed up and threatened to devour him. So, he kept his distance. As long as he stuck to business and didn't let things get personal, he could handle it. He could talk about relationships and spiritual things when it pertained to other people, but there was a reticence about him when it came time to reveal his own demons.

Very few people truly knew him. His parents, Alex, Prudie,

and Tom knew the whole story, but other than that, he still felt the whispers from time to time. He saw the look on Cynthia's face when he introduced Sarah. It continued to amaze him how misunderstandings and youthful mistakes could come back to haunt.

Alex's approval paved the way for his success in the real estate business, but events in Jared's past were partly what had kept him from law school. At one time, he'd considered a career in law enforcement, like his friend, Tom. He'd even considered the FBI. It was the fear of his lie being found out that kept him from pursuing it.

When he drove back to the beach house on Friday afternoon, he felt the urge to pull down the road that led to Pilot Oaks. He slowed as he passed the white frame house that had been his childhood home, and when he got past that, continued to the mansion. He simply sat in his car in the driveway, looked across the manicured lawn down to the summerhouse, and thought about Sarah. It surprised him when he felt a smile lift his lips. He thought about their walks on the beach and the way he felt comfortable with her like he hadn't with anyone in a long time – well, anyone but Prudie and Tom – and Alex.

Probably because she hasn't heard. His countenance faded when the thought crossed his mind. Who would be the lucky person to tell all? He wondered what she would think if she knew. When she knew.

SARAH HAD ARRIVED HOME LATE on Thursday night after a twelve-hour drive with stops only for Oliver's walks and to go through drive-thru restaurants for meals and snacks. For some reason, she didn't want to drag this trip out. She wanted to get home, get her stuff packed, and be back in South Carolina within a week. That was her personal goal. Her parents thought she would probably stay a couple of weeks, but unless she changed her mind, in a week her new address would be Murrells Inlet, South Carolina.

The days she spent in the real estate office had been wonderful. Oh, she was still confused about a lot of what they did there, but everyone accepted her and bent over backwards to help her get settled in. It was hard to leave when she felt like she was just getting the hang of things. Jared had been so patient. The office he had given her, Alex's old office, was handy to his, and when she was out of sight for a half-hour, his face would appear in the doorway to check on her. He made sure she wasn't confused about anything. "All you have to do is ask." His smile seemed to reach all the way into his eyes every time he looked at her.

She had a lot of time to think on that trip back to Kentucky. She made mental "pros and cons" lists all the way home.

"Pros – his eyes; his smile; his . . . the whole package – very handsome; successful in business; active in church; fun; compassionate; good manners; Ollie likes him . . .

Okay, she was really reaching now . . .

"Cons – drawing a blank; still blank; well, don't really know much about him; is he only interested in me to keep the business intact?"

With that last thought, her heart sank. It was true . . . she didn't know much about him. Was he as good as he seemed to be? He indicated that Uncle Alex had pointed him in the right direction, which could mean that he had been in some kind of trouble at one point. Were there consequences involved, or was it a youthful indiscretion that, while painful at the time, was just something that happened that taught him a lesson? Her heart told her that it wouldn't matter . . . but her head had her worried.

SHE PULLED into the drive of her little house with a sigh. Oliver had been asleep in the backseat, but he woke up when the car stopped. He was excited to be home, with his stuff, in his yard, in his house. But where was the sand?

Sarah laughed as the excited pup jumped out of the car and went straight to the backyard fence. He had run on sand so much that he seemed to want to roll in the grass . . . grass that needed to be cut, she thought with a groan. Somehow, she had thought maybe the vacation fairies would have come and mowed her yard for her, but they hadn't, and obviously, it had been rainy here while she was at the beach soaking up the sun.

"I guess I know what I'll be doing tomorrow." She called her mom to let her know she was home and that she would come by the next day—after the grass was cut.

She called Lucy next. "Luce! I'm home!"

"Yay! Is it too late to come over? I can't wait to hear all about it."

Sarah looked at the clock over the kitchen sink, 9:08 pm. She was exhausted, but still keyed up. Maybe a Lucy-fix was what she needed to wind her down. "Sure, Luce, come on over. I've got digital pictures, and fudge from one of the candy stores at Pawley's Island."

"Fudge and a slide show of your summer vacation . . ." Lucy giggled. "I can't wait to see them, especially if you've got pictures of those eligible bachelors you told me about. See you in a couple of seconds." She hung up before Sarah had a chance to say "goodbye."

Sarah handed Lucy a couple of bags to carry in when she got out of the car. With her help, they made short work of Sarah's gear. Within minutes, it was all brought in and put away. Lucy was one of those people with endless energy and one of those people who couldn't stand to put off until tomorrow what could be done today, or in this case, tonight.

When a load of laundry was put in the washer, her clothes hung up, and her toiletries put away, Lucy rubbed her hands together and said, "Okay, what about those pictures?"

"Okay, Mom." Sarah grinned at her with friendly disgust. If Lucy hadn't come over, she would have gone straight to bed – even if she couldn't sleep – slept late in the morning, and would probably have still had unpacked suitcases staring back at her at bedtime tomorrow night.

"Hey, I know you, girl. You always put off doing anything you consider unpleasant." Lucy flicked Sarah on top of the head as she started up her laptop to hook up her phone and look at the pictures.

The first few photos were of the condo and the beach, and most of them featured Oliver. When they got to pictures of Pilot Oaks, Lucy gasped, and Sarah sighed.

"And you came back?" Lucy laughed. Now maybe she could begin to understand Sarah's decision to relocate to South Carolina.

There were pictures that she had taken when her family came down, one of which included Jared. When she got to that one, she was mesmerized by his eyes. Those dark brown eyes seemed to gaze straight into her soul. It had been snapped out on the patio, the twins and Oliver center stage, but Jared, as he sat and talked to her dad, had looked up and smiled brightly at her when he saw her. He hadn't known she had her phone in her hand. He had just turned when he realized she stood there and simply smiled at her, and the expression was caught as she snapped the picture.

"Okay, Sarah, everyone in that picture, I know, except for that one." Lucy pointed specifically to Jared and gave Sarah that "this better be good" look that made Sarah shy, for some reason.

Sarah finally dragged her eyes away from the eyes of the

man in the picture. She blushed. "That, uh . . . that's Jared Benton. He's our business partner."

Lucy just stared at Sarah, her jaw slack. "Business partner. Uh-huh. I'm gonna say it again --- and you came *back*?"

Sarah quirked an eyebrow at her best friend. "Not for long."

THE DAYS SPENT in a busy real estate office taught her one thing about long-distance home sales. She needed help. As soon as she finished her yard work the next morning, she called Wayne Realty and arranged for a realtor to come over the next day and look over the house to put together a listing. The real estate market in this small town wasn't exactly booming – it was definitely a buyer's market – which was fine. She just wanted to unload it so she could get on with her life. The money didn't mean nearly as much to her, now, as it would have before.

She hated to admit it, but she was almost glad, in the cold light of day, that Lucy had insisted she unpack and put things away while she was there the night before. The adage, "many hands make light work," was certainly true in this case. Sarah loved to decorate, loved to arrange things artfully, but the general day-to-day de-clutter and routine housework was not her favorite thing. There was always something more fun to do: a new piece to play on the piano, email to check, important research on the Internet, and the list went on. Her mother had always despaired of her ever being a good housekeeper. Her standard reply was, "I'm not a housekeeper, I'm a musician," which did not shut her mother up.

As she drove through town to her parents' house, Sarah felt a twinge of regret as she passed familiar landmarks. There was the corner grocery store. She remembered looking through the glass of the deli counter while the grocer sliced meat and cheese and usually slipped her a bit of a piece while her mom wasn't watching. She thought he was ten feet tall, but from all accounts, he was average height, at best.

The church she had attended all her life was there, on the right. A white steeple reached to the sky. When she was about ten years old, the church had moved from the small building by the cemetery to the new, "modern" building closer to town. She knew every inch of the building. The choir room, where the seldom-worn robes hung, the double classroom where she spent her youth days.

She had spent her whole life here, except for her four years in college, and then she was here most weekends. Was she doing the right thing? This was home. In South Carolina, her decision seemed logical. Was it the allure of something different? Now, at home, those fears and doubts crowded in.

As she pulled into her parents' driveway, she was glad to see that they didn't have company. She wanted to spend time with her sister and her family, but she needed some "mom and dad" time alone. She was putting the car in gear when she heard her cell phone begin to vibrate.

When she looked at the screen, she felt a blush creep up her neck and into her cheeks.

"Hello?" She couldn't help but smile. "How are things in South Carolina?"

"They'll be better when a certain person gets back."

"Hmmm . . . I wonder who you could possibly mean?" She wondered, even as she teased, about the quiet sadness in his voice, and her heart leapt at the sound of his laughter.

"Very funny. I was on my way home from work and had a sudden urge to drive down the road to Pilot Oaks, and thought I'd call you while I was here at the summerhouse. Everybody at the office missed you today." His usual buoyant voice grew quiet.

"Thank everybody at the office for me, will you?" Sarah

hoped that he meant that *he* missed her. "Anything going on I should know about?"

"Not really. It was just really quiet today." He paused and cleared his throat. "When will you be back? I couldn't remember what you told me."

Sarah smirked into the phone. She had told him that she hoped to be back in a week. "Remember, I told you a week."

"Oh, yeah. That'll get you back in plenty of time to help get ready for the big open house day." When he said that, she felt that she heard a glimmer of humor in his voice.

"So, you just want me back to help with the grunt work, huh?" She teased him. As she smiled into the phone, she hoped desperately that her mother wouldn't look out and see her car in the drive yet.

"Of course! It's what we do, remember?" He laughed when he heard her corresponding "humph." "By the way, I got the papers back on your house this morning."

"Great! Don't I need to sign something? If I need to before I can get back, you could fax them to me and I can get them back to you." She felt herself sitting up straighter as she bounced a little in her seat. She stilled and paused a minute. "You called me at a good time, Jared."

"Why's that?"

"I wondered, for a bit, if I had made the right decision . . ."

"Do you think you are doing the right thing?" When he asked, she could hear traces of worry in his voice.

"I do. Just now, as I drove through town, I kept seeing the familiar people and places that have meant so much to me, and I wondered how I could possibly leave it."

"I can understand. What changed your mind?" The relief in his voice was evident.

"Well, there's the thought of a house right on the beach . . ." She laughed when she heard a laugh on his end as well. "I also realized these places aren't going anywhere. I can come back any time I want to."

"I'd like to see your hometown someday."

"I'd like to show it to you." Yes, she would like that very much.

"It's a date, then. Now, when did you say you were coming home?"

"I'll be home next Thursday night, okay? Listen, I'd better go. I saw Mom check out the window, and I've been spotted. Thanks for listening, Jared."

"Any time, Sunshine. Talk to you later?"

He had seemed as reluctant to end the conversation as she was.

"Yeah. Talk to you later," and she ended the call.

A BEAUTIFUL SUNSET all but ignored to his left, Jared drove to his beach house, the conversation with Sarah fresh on his mind. He could imagine that it would be hard to just pull up stakes and move to a place full of strangers. He'd done it several times, as a kid, and he knew he didn't want to do it anymore. It was hard to imagine the kind of life she and her family had led. They had lived in the same community, had all gone to the high school her grandparents attended, and had a lifetime of memories. They had generations of friends and family right there. To leave that would have to be hard, even if it felt like the right thing to do.

He said a little prayer for Sarah as he drove. He hoped that he had been able to encourage her just a little. In his experience, life didn't just happen. If it was meant to be, in God's own sweet time, it would happen.

CHAPTER NINETEEN

"Hey, sweetie." Her dad hugged her as he ushered her in the door. "I thought I saw your car in the driveway. Rest well last night after the drive?"

Sarah laughed as she sank onto the barstool at the kitchen island and took the cup of coffee offered by her mother. "Thanks, Mom. I needed some more coffee!" She took a long swig of the sweetened liquid. She still had to have two spoons of sugar in her coffee – everybody said she'd grow up one of these days. "Yeah, I rested great, finally. Lucy came over as soon as I called her. She just had to get all the details, after we got everything completely unpacked and the laundry going. You know how she is. You'd never know I'd been gone unless you looked in the refrigerator!"

"Lucy is quite a whirlwind, isn't she? See, other people like things neat and tidy, too!" Her mom had finally come to grips with the realization that Sarah was just not the housekeeper she had attempted to raise, but Sarah knew she couldn't resist a good-natured dig every once in a while.

"Yeah, well. I showed her the pictures of the beach, the house, and some of you guys that I took while you were there.

161

Wanna see?" She raised her brows in question as she pulled out her phone and held it up.

"Sure! Let's go in the office and hook it up to the computer. I don't have glasses strong enough to see them on that little screen." Dad led the way down the narrow hallway as he adjusted his bifocals.

As Sarah once again watched the slideshow of pictures from South Carolina, she noticed her mother's eyes cut toward her as she was obviously struck, as was Lucy, by the picture that caught Jared's expression.

Looking straight at the monitor, Mom twitched her lips. "Good picture of Jared, don't you think, Robert?"

It was the last picture in the slideshow, and Sarah found herself lost in his eyes. *Did he really look at me like that?* She shook herself out of her reverie when she heard her dad's voice.

"Will you be here for a few weeks to get packed up and ready to move?"

"No, I really need to get back next week. The big open house —you know, the one where they actually have open houses at all the properties listed at one time —is six weeks from tomorrow, and I really want to be there to help with the preliminary work."

Plus, she just plain wanted to get back. *Wonder if tomorrow would give her enough time?*

"Oh, I had hoped to have you a 'going away' party before you left, but I don't know if that will give us time." Mom sounded a little hurt and curious at the same time.

"I'll see everybody I need to see before I leave." Sarah turned to her dad. "Oh, and Lucy said she would go with me to help me move and spend a couple of weeks with me for her vacation."

"Good. I would rather you didn't make that trip alone, especially with a load. How much of your furniture will you take?

"Not much. I figure I'll get more appropriate stuff down there. I would like to take my piano, but I may have to leave it with you for now, if that's all right? I can always get an electronic one down there." That was the only regret she had. She would have to leave her one family heirloom behind.

"We can probably find room for it, if you'd like to leave it here." It was his mother's piano. Sarah's grandmother wasn't sentimental about a lot of things like Sarah was, but that piano and music in general, was a bond between grandmother and granddaughter that had only grown over the years. Dad winked at her.

"I, um, might have a few other things I might let you store for me, if you wouldn't mind." Sarah twisted her lips sheepishly. "I have some keepsakes that I don't want to get rid of, but don't necessarily want to move all the way to South Carolina, either – at least not right now."

"Are we talking high school awards and birthday cards here?" Her mother sighed when Sarah nodded in the affirmative. "How many boxes?"

"Well . . . a few?" Sarah raised her eyebrows and shrugged as Mom grimaced.

Sarah's last Sunday at her home church was more difficult than she had anticipated. Of course, all the little old ladies made a fuss over her, that surely down in South Carolina she could find her a nice young man, to which Sarah simply rolled her eyes. "I'm not going down there to find a husband. I'm going down there to work in a real estate business." She shook her head when they just patted her on the arm.

Her students from the high school, especially her choral students, were teary and dramatic over the whole thing, but after all the busybodies left, and they stood around to talk, her pastor helped her put it all in perspective.

"You know, Sarah, I read a book recently about living our

dreams. The author says that when we're faced with our dream, after we've decided to go for it, we can expect opposition, and sometimes from those close to us. Now, you seem to have a good support system of those closest to you, but you can expect that there will be many that won't understand why you would pack up and relocate. I'm proud of you, Sarah. I can tell you've prayed about it, and you seem to have a peace about your decision."

She looked at the pastor appreciatively, wondering how he could have known about the dreams that this move would fulfill. "I really do. It's almost as if I've already moved there – like South Carolina is more home than this is now."

"Are you sure there's not some young man out there waiting for you?" The pastor's wife teased her gently.

Sarah wondered if her intuition had been gained by osmosis, living with her husband. Had her mother or sister said something? Rather than come right out and lie about it, she decided to hedge. "Well, I don't know that he's actually 'waiting' for me, but I did meet someone. Pray for me?"

MOM PREPARED a big Sunday dinner and invited the whole family over for lunch so that Sarah would have a chance to see her family one more time before she left. Her grandmother was there, along with her aunts, uncles, cousins, and their families, the pastor and his family, and Lucy.

Sarah decided to head home after the "company" left, and she could tell her parents were ready for their regular Sunday afternoon nap. As she opened her door, her cell phone vibrated in her pocket. In nervous anticipation, Sarah looked at the screen and smiled broadly when she saw "J. Benton" on the caller-ID. She hadn't really expected to hear from him until closer to time for her to leave.

"Hey! What's going on at home?" Sarah knew there was an excited trill in her voice that couldn't possibly escape Jared's ears.

"You sound awfully chipper this afternoon. Haven't changed your mind, have you? Wait a minute – did you just ask what was going on at home?"

"Yep, I did. And you did not answer my question, Jared Benton." She giggled a little.

"Well, let's see. A dark cloud has hovered over the whole area since about, oh, Thursday. I think the weather man has predicted that the sun won't come out until about next Thursday?" The relief in his voice was audible in his laugh.

"Better watch out—those kinds of predictions could be bad for business, you know."

"Can't have that, now, can we? Hey, what can I do to help get you ready to move in? Do you need to stay in a condo for a few days until you get furniture and all? Or hey, you and Lucy could stay at my place . . . 'course that wouldn't look too good, would it?"

Sarah blushed, even though Oliver was her only audience. "No, that probably wouldn't be a good idea. A condo for a couple of nights might be good, if there's one available. I know how busy it is this time of year. Do you think it'll be a problem?"

"No, I don't think so. We usually have a few properties that don't show up when the "no vacancy" sign goes up on the website. Let me take care of it, okay? And Friday night, I thought maybe you, me, Lucy, and Tom could run up to Myrtle Beach and take in a show or something. How does that sound? If you're not too tired, that is."

"Friday sounds great! Wouldn't it be funny if the two matchmakers in our lives made a match themselves?" She laughed. "I'll call on the way home and let you know when we'll get in on Thursday. Do you want to leave a key in the after-hours box for me?" She couldn't help but hope he would offer to meet them, but refused to count on that. After all, he might have other plans, she told herself. No need to get her hopes up at this point.

"Sarah, I'll meet you at the condo. Just give me a call, and I'll tell you which one to go to." His voice was quiet but demanding. This was a man used to being obeyed. "I miss you."

"I . . . miss you, too, Jared." Why did she suddenly feel like an awkward teenager? She was an adult. She had a Master's Degree in Music Education, she owned her own home, she had made the decision to move over seven hundred miles from home. And yet the lump in her throat told her that this feeling fluttering through her body wasn't a bad thing.

"Call you in a couple of days?" He sounded anxious.

"Sure." The fluttering she felt started to feel like champagne bubbles flowing through her bloodstream. Champagne never felt like this, though. Gladness felt like this. She was glad. Glad that it was his idea. He had asked permission to call her. Was this how it felt to be well and truly courted? Or was she reading more into it than she should?

When they finally hung up from their conversation, Sarah threw herself into an overstuffed chair in her living room and just stared. Had it been only weeks since she had sat in this very room wallowing in self-pity that a former love had passed her over for someone else?

She felt a paw on her knee. Oliver sat at her feet and looked at her with that lopsided stare as if to figure out what was wrong with her. Sarah just laughed at his expression. "Oh, Ollie, what have we gotten ourselves into?"

CHAPTER TWENTY

*M*onday morning dawned clearly on the shores of South Carolina, the crash of the surf breaking the morning stillness and awakening the wildlife.

Jared had gotten up at sunrise to run on the beach and have some quiet time before the tourists took over his area of the beach. He hadn't slept well for a while, not since Alex died, actually. Sometimes the responsibility for the business weighed heavily on him. Alex had placed so much confidence in him – more confidence than he had in himself. So many people depended on his decisions for their livelihood. No one would know that it bothered him a little. But now Sarah would be here beside him.

The mental image he had of her as she walked along the beach, hair whipped into a mahogany frenzy, dog by her side, made him happy. She would depend on him, just like the others in the office, but it felt different. It was a different kind of dependence. She knew very little about the business, but he could tell that she was the kind who would dive right in and take it on like a pro.

He had prayed for someone like her to come into his life.

Whatever the past was, he knew that God would eventually send to him the woman He meant for all time. Many days he had almost given up on God's provision. He had been on more fix-up dates than he wanted to count, and it wasn't for lack of interest in him with the female of the species. He had asked a few women out, some of the dates had been okay, and some had been disasters. He found that women who pursued men tended to want things to go further on the first date than he was comfortable with.

Not that his upbringing had been the strictest as far as that went, but his dad had drilled into him from an early age that a man takes responsibility for his actions, and that included his actions with women. He came to realize, as a young man, that a guy didn't fool around physically unless he was prepared to commit both emotionally and spiritually. He had learned that the hard way.

Sarah was a special girl. He could tell that she had been sheltered, and that was part of her appeal. He wasn't anxious to break down those barriers—more likely he was anxious to know if she could consider someone like him—someone that, as far as the general population knew, would be considered "damaged goods."

"God, help me know how to approach this. As soon as people know she's here to stay and know that I'm interested in her, she'll hear the whispers. I've kept it all inside for so long, I don't know how I can ever explain to her what happened back then . . ." Jared hung his head as he sat there on the sand. When he looked up, the sun had peeped over the horizon. It almost blinded him. The roar of the surf seemed to still, momentarily. It gave him a sense of peace that he hadn't expected.

It was as if God stood right there beside him. Jared, you know I love you . . . just be still and know that I AM GOD.

SARAH WAS in the midst of a dream.

She saw Pilot Oaks again, but this time in its current state of repair. She rushed from room to room. She looked for something, but what? She was in a hurry, but couldn't move fast enough. Each time she came to a closed door, another door down the hallway opened, and as she got to that door, it closed, and another one down the hallway opened.

Frustrated, and about to give up, she looked to the top of the stairwell and saw a man with dark brown eyes. She had never seen him before, but something deep inside of her knew Him. He simply stood there and looked at her. He held his hand out, and gestured for her to come to Him. When she did, He took her hand in His, led her down the stairs and then out of the house. When they went out of the house, He took her to the beach, where the waves crashed all around them.

Suddenly, the brown-eyed man stopped and gazed intently at her, and then held His hand over the water. The waves calmed, and a sense of peace came over her as she heard a voice say to her, "Be still."

And with that, she awoke.

She was startled to see that she was in her own bedroom. The curtain blew in the breeze above her bed, and the sun streamed in the east window. She lay there a few minutes, not sure what all this meant. She had made her decision to change jobs, relocate, and leave her family and all that was familiar— and she felt good about all that.

Jared? She didn't know. She knew she felt something for him, and she thought maybe he did for her, but what did she really know about him – about his past? She had been taught not to hold a person's past against him, but then what did she know of a total stranger's life experiences? And that's what Jared was, basically. A total stranger.

"God? What do you want to tell me here? I've known the verse 'be still and know that I am God' since I was a kid. I know

I didn't exactly exhibit my spiritual ears when I began to make the decision to move, but You got my attention. Is he the one you have for me? I'm a little scared of how I feel when I'm around him. I want—no, I will depend on you to give me that peace that I can't even understand. I know you love me, and you want the best for me. If it isn't Jared, then please let me know. Please."

Tears trickled down her cheeks as she finally sat up in her bed and reached for a tissue. When she reached over to see what time it was, her cell phone began to ring. When she glanced at the caller-ID, she shook her head. Through her tears, in flashing letters, she saw the familiar "J. Benton."

"Good morning." Sarah sniffed loudly, but her heart was glad.

"Sarah? Are you okay?"

"Yeah. Just a little quiet time before the day gets started, you know? Lots to do, not much time to do it." Her heart had been made tender by that early morning encounter with God. She sensed that his voice was softer, too.

"I understand. I forgot it was an hour earlier there. Sorry if I interrupted."

"You didn't. I was just about to get up, had leaned over to see what time it was when my phone rang. You timed it just right." She wanted desperately for him to know that she was glad he called.

"Good. Pretty day here. What about there?"

"Beautiful, what I've seen of it." She laughed quietly and then sighed. "I can hear the surf in the background there. I'll bet it's a banner day on the beach, isn't it?"

"Yes, it is. I wish you were here . . . to see it." He added that last part in a hurry, the rush not lost on Sarah.

"Me, too. I'll get to see it Friday morning, if I don't oversleep. Is everything all right? You seem a little . . . subdued." Was that too personal? Did she come on too strong? She was a little worried that he would get tired of being responsible for her. She lacked experience in so many areas of life, not the least of which was in relationships with men.

"I'm fine. Just a little quiet today. Hey, I can't be witty and charming twenty-four/seven can I, Miss Crawford?" He was beginning to sound more like himself.

"I don't see why not, Mr. Benton! Have a good run this morning?"

"Yeah. I think I'll have to get a dog like Ollie. That's incentive to run, isn't it? Naw, I was going to call you later today, but I just . . . well, I guess . . . I wanted to . . . I'll just be glad when you get back." He seemed to retreat once again.

"Um . . . Jared . . . I had thought about leaving on Wednesday if I can get my stuff together. Do you think that would work?" She hadn't really thought about it, not until this minute, but he didn't have to know that. "I figured that way I could spend a few days on the beach and learn my way around town with Lucy before I start work next Monday."

"Really? That would be great! And if you need more time with Lucy, that's not a problem. You'll need time to get settled into the house, shop for furniture, and such. Hey, would you like me to take you up to Myrtle Beach? There are more furniture stores to choose from and several antique stores."

She pulled her knees up under her chin and grinned with satisfaction as she heard the spark come back into his voice with her news. What a difference one day made. "Maybe we could do that this weekend, after we've scouted out the area and gotten the house keys. Can we get the condo for Wednesday night?"

"You could stay at Pilot Oaks for a few nights, 'til your house is ready. It wouldn't be so lonely with Lucy and Oliver both with you."

"Hmmm. You know, I think Lucy would like that. It might be the last chance to stay there before it gets turned into a bed and breakfast. I've still got my keys, too." She would give him an out on meeting them if he wanted one.

"Sarah . . . I will meet you out there. I don't like the idea of two women arriving without someone to at least check and make sure everything's okay. Don't worry; I won't make a nuisance of myself."

"Who's the nuisance? I just don't want you to feel like you have to baby-sit me, since I'll be there full-time." Her voice was more wistful than she wished it were.

Jared snorted into the phone. "Believe me, Sarah; I do not look upon you as a baby-sitting job." He fell silent.

She was quiet as well as she tried to think of a good comeback to lighten the mood. She was a total blank. Figured. Why, oh why can't I be smooth when it comes to these things?

"You're right; it wouldn't be smart for two lone women to show up at an estate on a dead-end street with no backup. And . . . I'll be glad to see you." Suddenly, she just couldn't hold it in anymore. "Jared, did you ever feel like you were just ready to get on with life, and that life just keeps holding you up?" Her question came out in a burst, her frustration evident.

Jared answered her with a contented sigh and a chuckle. "I miss you, Sarah. Life will be waiting for you right here on the beach. You just have to get here and start living it. Talk to you later?"

"Sure. Today and tomorrow are 'box-up-stuff' days, if I'm to get away by Wednesday." She was a little embarrassed at her outburst and tried to get back on more impersonal topics.

"Then I'll let you get to it. Have a good day, Sarah, and don't rush it. Remember, life really will be waiting for you right here." Jared's voice sounded almost as wistful as hers had earlier.

SARAH'S last few days in Kentucky whipped around her and passed her like a whirlwind. Her mom and dad said little when she told them that she wanted to leave on Wednesday instead of Thursday. They accepted, at least to her face, that she wanted some time with Lucy and to get settled in before she started to work on Monday.

Her sister Susan simply stared.

When Sarah asked, "what?"

Susan said, "nothing . . . I . . . no, I won't say a word . . . yet . . ."

To which Sarah replied by rolling her eyes.

She realized, after that, that her temper had gotten shorter with each day that she was away from what she now considered home – South Carolina. The staring of her sister had sent Sarah into a huff. She turned on her heel to carry a box to the trailer that could have waited, and when she came back, her mom and sister were busy with a box of dishes.

"Mom, Sis . . ." She paused when they looked up at her.

"Sweetheart?" Her mom answered calmly.

She grimaced and turned a little red. "I don't know what's wrong with me."

Mom and Susan looked at one another and smirked. Susan was the brave soul to face the lion in her den. "Apology accepted, little sister . . . and if you really want to know what's wrong with you, I think we could probably help you figure it out!"

Sarah looked at her sister beneath her lashes, a disgusted look on her face as she shook her head and threw her hands in the air. "Ugh." She refused to give in to them. She simply wanted to get on with her life. The life Jared had talked about in South Carolina. On the beach. With him. The more she thought about it, the more she realized that she got that way just about every day . . . an hour or so before she received a phone call.

Jared called her every day that she was in Kentucky, except

for the call she made to let him know that she was on her way down. She didn't ask him to call, and every day she wondered if it might be possible that he wouldn't. Either way, the flutter of uncertainty and fear had worn out its welcome by Tuesday.

"God," Sarah prayed as she tried to get a handle on her insecurity. "If he's the one you have for me, then I want to be pursued. I don't want to even wonder if I've tried to make things happen. Will that work? Am I asking too much?"

CHAPTER TWENTY-ONE

*T*he trip from Kentucky to South Carolina was uneventful. The late-model car she had bought a year earlier took the mountain roads well. She had a tiny trailer hitched behind to carry her most precious belongings. Anything she failed to pack for this trip, her parents or sister could bring in the fall.

Lucy had never been to South Carolina before, so she was a veritable chatterbox all the way. Sarah sighed as she thought of her solitary trip down the first time – just herself, Oliver . . . and God. Better enjoy the company, Sarah, she told herself. Solitude will be yours again once Lucy goes back home.

As they crossed the state line, Lucy turned in her seat, arms crossed, and stared at Sarah.

"What?"

"You know what. You still haven't told me anything about Jared except that he's your business partner, you went out with him a couple of times while you were there—business dinners only, and then there's what I've seen with my own eyes."

"And what's that?" Sarah kept her eyes on the road, but she was fully engaged in the conversation.

"That he's also incredibly handsome and has a killer smile. So . . . I've bided my time, waited until there was nobody around —well, except Oliver, and you don't count, do you, sweetie?" Lucy took time out to scratch under the furry chin that had wriggled its way between the front seats when his name was called. "So? Are you gonna fill me in or take the chance on me using my ultra-feminine wiles to capture this guy myself?"

Sarah glanced over at Lucy and laughed at her exaggerated batting eyelashes. "Okay, okay, what do you want to know?"

Lucy smiled gently, and her teasing tone turned serious. "I want to know what makes your eyes go all gooey when his name is mentioned or when you start staring off into space. I want to know what brings that little wrinkle between your eyebrows that you've had longer than I've even been around. I want to know what makes you blush at the oddest times. Oh, and one more thing."

Sarah glanced sideways at her best friend. "What's that?"

"Does he have a brother?"

JARED WAITED NOT SO PATIENTLY in South Carolina. When she called from Spartanburg, he was at her house with a cleaning crew that he had sent over to get things ready. He didn't want her to have to wait a day to move in once she found furniture. He was almost as excited as she. Now he knew what that phrase, "a kid in a candy store," means.

"Hey, Jared," Sarah said when he answered his cell. "How are things at home?"

"Great. Where are you?"

"Spartanburg. We've just made a quick stop for Ollie, and then we hope not to stop any more until we get to Pilot Oaks. I think we'll get there before dark. Do you want me to call you again when we get close, so you can meet us?"

He looked at his watch. "You'll be here in about four and a half hours. I'll be here. Call me if you have any trouble, okay? Have you had a good trip so far?"

"Yeah. The car was great, even through the mountains. Lucy's enjoyed the scenery, and the time has passed pretty quickly with her talking to me the whole way!" Sarah laughed.

Jared heard a muffled "Ow!"

"What happened?"

"Lucy just punched me on my arm."

He laughed. "Tell Lucy I can't wait to meet her. Be careful."

"I will, and don't worry; you can't get rid of me now. See you after a while," she said softly.

"I'll be here, Sarah."

"So?"

Sarah sighed as she put down the phone. "I wish I knew, Luce. It's like nothing I ever felt before. I mean, you know how it was with Marc. I thought he was the 'one.' But obviously, he wasn't. I thought he was the one God had for me, and when that fell apart, I was so confused. And now Jared. He's pretty special, and he makes me feel pretty special."

Lucy was quieter than usual. "I'll bet he smells really good, too, doesn't he?"

The laugh that burst from Sarah surprised both of them. "What?"

"His picture. He looks like a guy that would use really good cologne."

"You know, now that you mention it . . . he does smell really good." Sarah shook her head and looked over at Lucy. "I was getting too serious, huh?"

"Just a tad. Tell ya what. Don't tell me anything else. I want to see if my skills as your number one matchmaking friend have been compromised in any way, so I'll just keep my eyes open and see what I can see. Deal?"

"Deal. Because I don't really know what I could tell you right now, anyway."

"Just one question." Lucy's scheming smile was back, full-force.

"Just one?"

"Uh-huh. And you didn't answer it earlier. Does he have a brother?"

"Yes, who is married and has two children." Sarah laughed again at the look of disappointment on Lucy's face. "But, he has a friend who is an unattached police detective. Will that do?"

Lucy straightened in her seat. "Nicely. Tell me more about him."

Sarah made her way back onto the Interstate and toward Georgetown, Pawley's Island, and Pilot Oaks. "Well, he's about as much of a matchmaker as you, it seems. Both he and Jared take their turn on the 'most eligible bachelor' lists that the Junior League puts together each year."

"Sounds promising." Then her voice flattened as her left eyebrow went up. "What's wrong with him? There has to be something wrong with both of them if they're over thirty and haven't been snagged by now. I figure my chances are pretty slim."

Sarah shrugged and shook her head. "Not a thing, as far as I know. Still waiting for Ms. Right, perhaps?"

"Hmmm . . . I'll just wait and see for myself. Gotta be something. Hey, did I tell you about Janice and Bob?"

"No, you didn't."

"Well . . ." Lucy began, and Sarah took the opportunity to let her mind wander as all the juicy details about the love affair between the home economics teacher and the assistant football coach—people that she didn't care that much about—floated right over her head and out the open car window. She had other things, other people, that she would much rather think about.

"Jared, when you don't know what to do next, just do the next right thing."

Alex had given him that piece of advice years ago, and it had cropped up each time a major decision needed to be made. Another two years of law school or a business partnership with a seventy-five-year-old man? Tell the truth and hurt people unnecessarily or keep it to yourself and deal with it? It was a philosophy that he had carried with him all these years, and it had served him well. It wasn't always an easy truth, but it was one way to put things in perspective.

Today was the day that Sarah would come home. He had gone into the office, but he couldn't settle to anything. He touched base with all his key players, made arrangements for the crew at Sarah's house, checked on a couple of projects, and then headed over to Pilot Oaks to make sure everything was set for Sarah and Lucy tonight. He checked the food supply from when the family had been there the week before and picked up some milk, bread, and fruit for them to have in the morning. He felt like this was the next right thing.

He decided to give his mom a call, just to check in, and to kill a little more time. "Hey Mom, what's going on in DC?"

"Not much, Jared. Your dad's at a meeting at the church, and we're having some friends over for supper tonight. You remember General Warren and his wife, Estelle?"

"Was he stationed in Florida when we were there?" Jared tried to place the Warrens, people that he may have met once and would probably never see again.

"No, he was in Texas. You remember. He had a daughter that you had a crush on. Natalie, I think her name was. You know, I don't think she's married, either." Mary Benton chuckled when she heard her son sigh over the phone.

"Mom . . ."

"I'm sorry, son. I just want to see you happy. Is that a crime?"

She was so transparent. She was deeply in love with her two grandchildren, and her world would only be complete when she had grandchildren from all her children.

"Mom, I'm . . . I'm doing my best, okay?"

"You've met someone, haven't you?"

He held his phone out and looked at it, startled at his mother's question. How did she pick up on these things? He shook his head and grinned before getting up the nerve to take up the conversation again. "Mom . . . uh . . . maybe . . . how did you know?"

"Mother's intuition, dear. We have our ways. Will we get to meet her when we come down in a few weeks? Hmmm?"

"I suppose so. Actually, yes, you will. She's my new business partner." He decided that in this case, honesty was the best policy. Besides, there was no point in hiding it from her. She would drag it out of him eventually.

"How convenient! I can't wait to meet her! I'm sure you father will be glad, too." She sounded much happier than when he first called.

"I'd better get off here, Mom, and let you get to your dinner preparations. I'm busy tonight, too. Let me know what your plans are, so I can carve some time out for you, okay?"

"Yes, sir." Her giggle sounded much younger than her sixty years. She sounded just like his sister, and he could imagine her saluting him over the phone. "Sometimes you sound as much like a commanding officer as your father. Talk to you soon, son."

He chuckled as he put his phone away. He thought about his parents, and of the life they'd had just down the road from here. It had been a good time for their family. It was while they lived here that Jared finally found home. Dad away from the base was totally different from Dad always on call. It gave them all a chance to know a man that they hadn't met before. When he came home, here, he was truly home. When they lived here, Mom was more of a homebody than she had ever been. None of the "trying to keep up with the Joneses" mentality, rampant among some of the officers' wives on the base, seemed to touch them here.

It was while they lived here that they found the church just down the road. It created in him a habit that continued to this day. Oh, while he was away in college he kind of got away from church, but it was always there when he was ready. God never forsook him.

There was a time when he thought he'd been forsaken, but he soon found out that God hadn't moved. Jared Benton had.

He still had time on his hands before Sarah and Lucy were to arrive, so he walked down toward the summerhouse and the marsh. It was a good time, a good place to pray. No interruptions, no people distracting him from his task, which was to literally pick God's brain just a little bit.

"I'm content to wait, God . . . I'll wait for you to let me know what your plan is. I remember when Alex told me to do the 'next right thing.' It was a time in my life that I felt like you had deserted me. I know you never did, but you did seem far away. Right now, you're close in some areas, but awfully quiet in others. I trust you, Lord. You know how she makes me feel. Does she feel the same? I just have to know if she's the one you want for me, and I'll try really hard to be patient . . . and wait for a word from you."

CHAPTER TWENTY-TWO

*W*hen Sarah got out of the car in front of Pilot Oaks, a sigh of relief escaped Jared. He had held his breath without even realizing it. She was beautiful – somewhat disheveled, yes, her jeans and t-shirt wrinkled from travel, and her girlish ponytail slightly askew – but beautiful.

He had almost run to her car to open the door for her, but didn't want to scare her with too much attention. He walked briskly down the walk, knelt with a treat when Oliver came directly to him, and smiled as he rose and reached out for Sarah's hand. He pulled it to his lips and kissed that hand, conscious of the blush on her cheeks that rivaled the red of her t-shirt.

"I'm glad you're back." Jared gloried in her reaction, his confidence bounding. He hadn't expected to kiss her hand like a hero in a Regency romance, but once done, he found that it just felt right. What he really wanted to do was sweep her into his arms and kiss her, but he thought better of it when he looked over Sarah's shoulder at the perky little blonde who was watching them with acute interest.

"Me, too." Sarah's gaze seemed to be trapped in his. It thrilled him to see that she couldn't seem to tear her eyes away from his. An impatient tap on her shoulder brought them both back to reality in the form of Lucy as she waited, not so patiently, to be introduced.

"It's great to meet you, Lucy! I've heard a lot about you." Jared shook her hand.

"It's nice to meet you, too. I must say I haven't heard nearly enough about you!" She arched an eyebrow as Jared cut a glance at Sarah, who had bugged her eyes at her best friend to communicate with a glare that obviously meant "stop it!" Lucy glanced away.

Jared laughed at the silent interchange. He couldn't wait to get Lucy and Tom together. He thought they would hit it off perfectly.

"WHAT DO you think about this one?" Sarah arched her brow at Jared and wore a saucy grin as they stood and stared at a miniature floral-patterned sofa.

"You like this one?" He raised one eyebrow in incredulous disbelief. If she liked it, he would keep his mouth shut. He struggled to not show how he really felt about it, but he was obviously not successful. He sat on it, reached for her hand, pulled her down beside him, and turned his head to look at her with a quizzical expression. "Do you really like this one?"

Sarah paused before she laughed and then turned a little red. "No, to be honest, I wouldn't be caught dead with it in my house, but it was worth it to see the look of horror on your face!"

Jared twisted his mouth in a grin that admitted he'd been had and kept her hand clasped in his as they sat there and laughed together. He felt like rejoicing when her breath caught. Better stay on safe topics, for now. He squeezed her hand and tilted his head in the direction of laughter across the store. "Looks like Lucy and Tom have hit it off. They're over there test-driving the massage chairs."

"Lucy has always been fascinated by those things." Sarah looked once more across the store. "Oh! Let's go look at that one." She sprang from the sofa and pulled at Jared's hand to lead him to a soft, oversized, blue leather sofa.

Jared much preferred this one, both for looks and comfort. "I like it." He sat beside Sarah on leather that was so soft it felt like silk. This one had definite possibilities.

When Sarah found the sofa of her dreams, she declared the day an early success, and the others agreed wholeheartedly – especially Jared.

THE REST of the day passed in a pleasant blur. The girls had beaten the men at miniature golf – of course they insisted that they let them win – and the dinner show at the Dixie Stampede was a treat like Sarah had never had opportunity to enjoy before. She was especially touched by the patriotic climax of the show, and from the expressions on everyone else's face, they were as well.

On the drive home, Sarah leaned her head back onto the comfortable leather of the front seat of the SUV. Lucy and Tom were enjoying a lively conversation in the back seat, but Jared drove quietly, a bemused expression on his face.

He reached for her hand. "What are you thinking about?"

She could feel her heart race, but in a good way. What was she thinking? She was thinking about how natural it felt to have his fingers curled around hers. About how her hand seemed to naturally turn and find comfort in his clasp. After a pause, she turned her head and looked at him, letting her cheek rest on the soft leather. "What am I thinking? I guess about what a great day it's been, of how it feels good to already have friends here that I can count on, that I love the way you've made Lucy and me feel accepted . . ." She glanced back with a chuckle at the animated conversation that had Lucy completely oblivious to anything Sarah and Jared might have in mind. ". . . and how much I'm enjoying that we've effectively distracted Lucy with your friend Tom!"

Jared chuckled, his eyebrow raised with good humor. "I didn't just do it for Lucy, you know." He gave her a sly look and twisted his lips in a mischievous smile as he massaged her wrist with his thumb. "Do you think Oliver will need a walk when we get you home?"

"You know, I think he just might, at that." Sarah felt the flush creep up her face and was thankful for the darkness of the vehicle.

LUCY AND TOM sat on a large swing at one end of the front porch while Jared and Sarah took Oliver down to the edge of the water. Oliver ran along the waves and chased after the ball that Jared had picked up next to his leash. They walked without talking, hand in hand, stealing occasional glances at each other.

Oliver, finally tired out from the burst of energy he'd greeted them with when he saw Jared and knew that he was in for some play time, flopped down on the beach in front of them, forcing them to stop. Jared turned Sarah toward him and took her hands in his. "I really had a good time today. Could we do this again sometime?"

"I'd like that." Sarah gazed up at him. When she squeezed his hands back, she felt something pass between them. Did he feel it, too?

He broke eye contact for a second. "I've got some business to take care of tomorrow, but will I see you at church on Sunday? I'd really like to see you, Sarah." His look of almost longing, or regret, in his eyes made her look at him gently. It was as if he already regretted the plans he had for Saturday and would love to make an excuse to break them.

"We'll be there. Lucy and I had planned a lazy day at the beach tomorrow, to rest up before the big move-in day on Monday! Would you and Tom like to come over for lunch Sunday afternoon? I've invited Prudie, too." Sarah looked at him slyly. "Hmmm . . . on second thought, we could probably get some pretty good stories about the two of you if you aren't there."

"Do you honestly think Prudie would let a little thing like our presence there stop the stories from being told? Come, now. We'll be there if only for self-preservation." He turned serious and pulled her a little closer. "Honestly, Sarah, I can't remember when I've enjoyed a day more. Thank you."

"You're welcome, Jared." She was mesmerized by the moonlight, or was it the glow in his eyes?

She felt his hand reach up to brush away the hair that blew into her face, and then, in an instant, he leaned down and kissed her tenderly. It was a brief kiss, so gentle that she barely had time to realize what had happened. She gazed up at him, lips parted slightly in a sigh, and reached up to touch his face

Tired of being ignored, Oliver decided that it was time to go home and started wriggling between them.

"I guess we'd better get back up the hill, hadn't we?" Jared still held her in the circle of his arms.

Sarah wasn't any more ready to move than he, but she nodded, then chuckled nervously. "I suppose so."

As they walked back to the house, Oliver in tow, Jared put

his arm around Sarah's shoulders and drew her closer to him, and she put her hand tentatively on his waist. Within sight of the house, but still in shadow, Jared stopped for a minute, tugged her closer, and kissed the top of her head. Before he let her go, he put his hands on each cheek and then threaded his fingers through her silky hair before he brushed her lips with his once more.

As he pulled his hands from her face, he reached down and took her hand in his, kissing it, then weaving his fingers through hers. Sarah knew she wasn't ready for an interrogation and sensed that Jared wasn't ready for the third degree they would get from both Tom and Lucy if they were to see them wrapped in one another's arms.

SARAH CLOSED the door behind her and sighed. She headed slowly up the stairs and thought about the walk on the beach and about the days to come.

Tonight, she, Lucy, and Oliver had Pilot Oaks all to themselves. Prudie wanted to come out so that they wouldn't be alone in a strange place, but Sarah told her that she would like for them to try it on their own. She invited her for lunch on Sunday to meet Lucy.

She felt well cared for. Rainey Thompson had called when she knew they were in town and told her to be sure to bring Oliver over any time she needed to, and she just wanted to check on her. She was a mom. She told Sarah she knew how she would feel to know her baby chick was alone in a strange place.

She took one more turn through the downstairs of the house to turn off lights and check the doors. It was quiet. Lucy had gone upstairs to prepare for bed, and she thought about her decision to move here, full-time. It was a good move. She thought about Jared, and the way she felt toward him. Those were good thoughts, too. But where would it lead?

Pausing, she sat on the bottom step for a minute to pray before she went up the stairs. She looked up, knowing that God was there with her . . . He was everywhere . . . and sometimes she just needed to look around for him, like if she tried hard enough, she could see him as he floated somewhere above her.

"Lord, I know you're here. I feel you. I know you were in my move. But, what about Jared? I need your help here, Lord. I don't know if I've ever felt this way. No, I know I've never felt this way. It's like I can't get enough of his company, and yet, I don't really know him. Is there something wrong with me? I think he would like to pursue a relationship with me, but he seems to pull away, too. Help us both, Lord. I've prayed for someone for a long time. I have a feeling he has, too."

Sarah thought of the verse she had claimed since high school. Psalms 37, verse four –Delight yourself in the Lord, and He will give you the desires of your heart. For some reason, it always made her happy. Then there was the passage in James 1 that always came back to her –Consider it pure joy, my brothers, whenever you face trials of many kinds, because you know that the testing of your faith develops perseverance.

"Thank you, Lord. I know the trials aren't over. I know you've still got decisions out there for me to make, and I have to depend on You."

She made her way up the stairs and sighed as she passed slowly down the hallway and Lucy's open door. When she reached her bedroom, Sarah took off her earrings and necklace and put them in her makeup case.

"You know, I would say, if I didn't know better, that my best friend didn't just inherit a big house and a business; she inherited a whole lot more." Lucy stood in the doorway. Her saucy tone faltered when she saw Sarah's expression. "Okay, young lady. This is me. Your best friend. Are you ready to spill yet?"

When Sarah made no move to fill her in, but instead continued to stare at herself in her vanity mirror, Lucy put her hands on her hips and shook her head.

"Something tells me that our 'girls' nights out' are numbered."

CHAPTER TWENTY-THREE

"*A* day at the beach was just what the doctor ordered." Lucy stretched as she lazed on an oversized towel on the private stretch of beach down the hill from Pilot Oaks. "And this beach is to die for." It was a beautiful day with just a hint of haze in the sky that made it less bright on the eyes and enough breezes to make the heat and humidity bearable.

"Amen to that. Although the beach where my little house is in Murrells Inlet is nice, too. We should probably go over and check on things later this afternoon. Did I show you Jared's house when we went over there? It's amazing. The funny thing is I don't think he likes it all that much." Sarah's mind went back to the Sunday afternoon when her family was still here. "It was like he just bought it as an investment, or to keep up the appearance of a wealthy, single guy."

Lucy didn't answer her. Sarah gazed out at the ocean, a half-smile on her face as she thought about the white frame house with rosebushes just down the road from where they were. She had noticed, when with Jared, that when they passed that house, he seemed to crane his neck every time to take in every inch of the property.

Sarah's wonder grew as she thought, once again, about the walk with Jared on the beach. Lucy hadn't been able to get more than "we had a nice walk" out of Sarah last night. She was, indeed, beginning to slip in the interrogation department.

"Sarah." Lucy's voice drifted in with the breeze that blew off the Atlantic. "Sarah!" Lucy tried again, but this time threw a flip-flop at her friend and giggled at the blush on Sarah's face as she realized that her mind had wandered . . . again.

"What?" Sarah was quick with her answer, a little irritable at the thought of being caught in a daydream.

"Girl, what's with you? If I didn't know better, I'd say you were back in tenth grade mooning over Jimmy Henderson in biology class." Sarah had to laugh at Lucy's reminder of those awkward days of crushes and acne. Sarah had the crush. Jimmy Henderson had the acne.

"Sorry. I guess I wandered off for a bit, didn't I?" She reached for her bottle of water. She wanted to find something, anything, to do to keep her busy.

"Wandered? That's an understatement, Sarah. This is me, Lucy, remember? We've told each other everything since ninth grade chorus. You are the one who got up the nerve to tell me I couldn't sing, and guess what, I'm still here! If that didn't run me off from being your best friend, nothing could." A comical expression graced Lucy's face, but there was a hint of seriousness in her words. "You know, I have noticed that it doesn't matter what the topic of discussion is, the subject always comes around to Jared Benton."

How could she put into words what she didn't really understand herself? Could she tell her that he made her feel like that tenth grader she teased about? As close as she was to Lucy, what would she think of her if she told her those innermost thoughts and feelings that alternately washed through her blissfully and confused her utterly? Sarah narrowed her eyes and twisted her lips into a grim half-smile as she realized that she didn't have to face any of this alone.

"Oh, Luce." Tears began to gather in her eyes as she tried to pull her thoughts together. Her emotions threatened to take control for the first time since she made the decision to pull up stakes and move to South Carolina.

"Hey, it's okay." Lucy seemed a little surprised at the emotions that bubbled to the surface, but still she waited and sat quietly. "What's really upset you? Is it Jared? Leaving home? I'm here for you. You know that."

Sarah sighed and grinned weakly at her friend, then wrapped her arms around her knees as she sat on the blanket. She bumped her shoulder into Lucy's shoulder in an attempt to lighten the mood before she started to talk.

"I guess it's everything, Luce. I don't know. I'm excited to be here, excited that something has finally happened in my life, and then on the other hand, I'm scared to death. You know change has never been a favorite of mine, but Lucy, I asked God to bring some changes to my life. It's like . . . oh, it's so hard to explain when I don't even really understand it myself." Sarah struggled with her thoughts and emotions that were at war within herself.

Lucy sat still a minute. She dug her fingers into the sand and sifted it through her fingers as she thought about what Sarah had said.

"I don't know why I didn't come to you first. You just seem so . . . I don't know . . . confident. I guess I wanted to figure it out on my own for a change."

Lucy leaned her chin on her arms, which she had stretched out over her knees as she sat on the beach towel. "Why do you think you're excited about this change?"

Sarah stared at the doodles she had created in the sand next to her. She should know by now that Lucy wouldn't just give her straight advice. She would make her think about it. She sighed again and forged ahead. "I think I'm excited because this is the first decision I've ever made, truly, on my own. It's like other big decisions have been made for me. When Marc and I . . . well, when that happened, I had no choice. And you know, I've liked not having to make those choices up to now, because I don't think I was ready before."

Lucy nodded encouragingly.

Sarah looked at her friend. "I think I'm also excited because I've met someone that I really like, and that makes me feel things that I've never felt before. Good things. I'm excited to think about a relationship with someone who hasn't known me since I was three." Sarah laughed as she thought about some of her more recent dates with guys that she'd known since Preschool Story Hour.

"Okay, you know I would love to continue that line of questioning, but I'll hold off." Lucy laughed and held up her hands when she saw the flash of humor on Sarah's face.

Sarah gave her a sheepish grin and then looked down at her hands. "I suppose now you want to know what scares me to death in all this." Her voice was almost so low that it was difficult to hear with the surf and the wind off the ocean.

"Hmmm . . . I guess I need to mix up my interrogation techniques. I'm becoming predictable. But yes, that's the next item on the agenda. What's wrong?"

"Would you believe all the same things? It scares me to make life-altering decisions. I wonder if I have enough experience to really make good decisions – especially the kind that affects other people. I wonder if I'm cut out for a totally new kind of job. I wonder why somebody like Jared would want to date me. I mean, he's so . . . so . . . you know . . . I mean have you looked at him?" Sarah's frustration tumbled out as she tried desperately to find the words to express how she truly felt.

Lucy looked at her friend in disbelief. "Sarah. You're kidding, right? Do you know how pretty you are?"

Sarah shook her head furiously. "Lucy, you're just saying that because you're my best friend and you want me to feel better."

"Uh, 'scuse me, girlfriend, but I also have eyes. What's wrong with the way you look?"

"I'm gawky, I have freckles, and who knows what color my eyes are. I like stuff that nobody else seems to like—well, except you."

"Okay, I think we may have our work cut out for us here. One, you're not thirteen, which is what you just described—you are not gawky. You have a great figure and if you could donate a few inches to me both in height and bust size, I'd be eternally grateful. Two, freckles? Please. Who are you, Jan Brady?"

Sarah laughed, which encouraged Lucy to go on. "Three, your eyes. They're hazel, dear. You know, that color that can change from blue to green to gray in mere seconds? I don't even want to hear about it. And then the stuff you like?" Lucy stopped. "The stuff you like is what makes you, you. The best friend a girl could have, and any man who can't handle what you have to offer is a lot less of a man than you need."

She put her hand on Sarah's shoulder and gave her a gentle shake. "Sarah, have you looked in the mirror lately? Why wouldn't someone like Jared want to go out with someone like you? I mean really. We'll get to Jared later. I think you've been dealing with some deeper things than what you look like, for goodness' sake. Sarah, do you think God wants you to be scared?"

"N-noooo. What do you mean?" This wasn't about whether she had secured the right prom date. This was real life.

"It always amazes me how all those scriptures we memorized in the youth group come back when you need them. Have you thought through some of those lately? Somehow, one just popped into my mind – Second Timothy, first chapter, seventh verse. Do you remember what it says?" Lucy probed.

"Second Timothy 1:7 . . . it's about fear, isn't it?" Sarah

thought a minute, and then pulled the words from the recesses of her mind. "For God has not given us the spirit of fear . . ."

". . . and timidity, but of power, love, and self-discipline . . ." they finished together.

"You got it. God doesn't want us to be fearful and confused, Sarah. That comes from us, not Him. You know that. You're just too close to it. If this were me about to face these changes – which, by the way, all seem to be good changes if you ask me – I would probably be a basket case and take months to decide and make you crazy in the meantime." Lucy took Sarah's hand and squeezed it hard to make her point.

Sarah looked over at her friend, a mist of tears in her eyes and a smirk on her face. "Lucy, you've never taken months to decide anything, but thank you. I thought I had worked through the fear part, but I guess a part of me is afraid to be happy . . . it's like I've conditioned myself to wait for the other shoe to drop, you know?"

"Yeah, I know. It's been a tough couple of years, but you've got some good things going on. It won't all be easy, and there will be some aspects of this change that might not go like you want it to, but you're not alone, you know. Remember that one verse you and I both claimed? From Psalm 37 – I've talked to more people that claim that verse – Delight yourself in the Lord and He will give you the desires of your heart," Lucy reminded her. "It sounds like a fun verse, doesn't it? Like if you do the right things, God will give you whatever you want? Ha! Not that simple! I've found out that it doesn't mean He'll do anything for us we ask, but that he will put the right desires in our hearts."

Sarah's eyes widened as realization dawned. She thought about all that had happened—and that included the job and Jared. Maybe this was God's way of showing her that He, God, called the shots and that He waited for her to allow Him to insert His desires into her heart. The decisions weren't hard to make. It was afterwards, when she had made the commitment to do it, that the doubts began to creep in, stalling her.

"Lucy, I'm glad you're here with me today. I think I needed to be with just you for a little bit. Sometimes it's nice to be reminded of where you've been and where you've come from, to realize how great it will be where you're going. Does that make sense?" Sarah scrunched her face in a frown.

"Makes perfect sense to me, girlfriend. Glad I could help." Lucy gently elbowed Sarah in the ribs. Then, she put her chin on her fist and leaned toward her as she batted her eyelashes and arched her eyebrows. "Now, about Jared. Care to share?" She gave Sarah her cheesiest grin as she waited expectantly.

"You are a bad, bad woman, Lucy Dixon." Sarah smirked at her as she shook her head in amazement.

"So, did Sarah suspect anything when you told her you had business to take care of today?" Tom didn't want to get on the wrong side of any argument that might come about as the result of Jared's deception.

"Not a thing." Jared grinned to himself as he thought about their walk on the beach the night before. "She said she and Lucy would spend today on the beach, and then we're supposed to go eat lunch with them after church tomorrow. I didn't tell her where my 'business' was taking place."

They were sitting on the porch of Sarah's Murrells Inlet house, waiting for a delivery truck. Robert had called Jared to make arrangements to have Sarah's piano shipped out to her. "She left it here with us, but if I know Sarah, she'll miss it. It's been like her right arm at times, Jared." That was all it took. Jared made a few calls, and the piano was on its way to South Carolina.

Tom laughed and stared at Jared, a comical grin on his face.

"What?" He was wary. He didn't like to think he was so transparent, but then he didn't want to evade the truth completely either.

"Oh, nothing. I figure you'll tell me what's going on in that hard head of yours eventually." He chuckled as Jared shifted a little uncomfortably in his chair.

"She's pretty special, isn't she, Tom?" Jared wanted Tom's approval for some reason. He'd never felt it important before now. He had always figured that his relationships were his own business, and he didn't bother Tom about his. Fair enough, right? But this was different . . .

Tom looked at Jared with a surprised expression on his face. "Apparently, you think so. And I have to agree. Are we getting old, or what? I can't even come up with a crack about her that would get you riled up."

Jared laughed out loud at the disgusted look on his friend's face. "Well, you may not have been trying, but you succeeded anyway." He relaxed, and then frowned a little as he shook his head. "I'm not sure whether to be happy about it or scared to death."

"What do you mean?"

"You know what I mean . . . Annabelle . . ." Jared looked at Tom and waited for it to sink in.

"Annabelle's gone, Jared. It's time you put it behind you. And anyway, what does that have to do with Sarah?" Tom seemed frustrated.

"As soon as some of the people around here know I'm interested in Sarah, you know what they'll be anxious to 'share' with her . . . in her best interest, of course," Jared said, full of frustration and dread. "I don't want her to have to deal with that."

"Then why don't you tell her your side of the story before she hears it from all and sundry—namely Cynthia—because you know she's just itching to be the one to 'share' with her. You can't carry this around with you forever, bud. If you think Sarah may be 'the one,' then you'd better do some serious praying about all that it means to have someone that close to you. Are you ready for that? I've heard it's quite a responsibility, but I've also heard – and would really like to test it one of these days – that it's worth it." Tom gave Jared a sidelong glance and a smile that lightened the lecture-like aspects of what he had said.

Jared spoke seriously. "I overheard a conversation between her mom and sister. She was engaged once. Don't know what happened." He had leaned forward in the porch chair, his fingers clasped together between his legs as he bowed his head.

"Well, obviously, she's not engaged now. I think I read somewhere, Second Timothy, I believe, that God has not given us the spirit of fear and timidity, but of power, love, and self-discipline. I think this is something you need to take up with Him and then with Sarah."

Tom paused. "She seems like a good girl, Jared. Not your run-of-the-mill debutante that hangs all over you and bats her eyelashes at you to get your attention. She also seems like someone who would understand. She's probably going through some of the same things. If she's been engaged, then at one time she thought she'd found the man she wanted to marry. She's probably got more doubts about you than you do about her. It's not all about you, you know. Are you willing to give up on a relationship with a woman that might just be the one God has for you, just to save yourself from some hurtful moments, some embarrassment? A lifetime of happiness versus a short time of discomfort? Girls like that are one in a million. I just hope there are two million girls out there, so that I can get the other one."

Jared's countenance lightened at his friend's words. "You're right, O Wise One." Jared twisted his lips as he looked over at his friend. "I needed that."

When they looked up, they saw a truck had backed up to the

front of the house, and then a uniformed delivery man walked up to the porch with a clipboard. "Mr. Benton?"

"That's me." Jared signed his name on the form attached to the clipboard.

"Your wife will sure be tickled to get her piano, I'll bet." The gentleman smiled from ear-to-ear. "And I'm glad you two are here to help move the heavy beast out of my truck and into the house."

"Well . . . she's not my wife . . . at least not yet." Jared handed him back the clipboard. He winked at Tom, then rubbed his hands together in anticipation. "Let's just get that piano unloaded, shall we?"

CHAPTER TWENTY-FOUR

*J*ared and Tom got the piano situated in the spot that he had heard Sarah say would be a perfect place for a piano someday.

Tom looked over at Jared when he heard a deep sigh resonate beside him. He laughed. "Wish you hadn't told Sarah you'd be gone all day?"

They'd been friends way too long. "Yeah. I wonder what they're up to tonight."

"Well, my man, I guess we could always call them up and see? I could probably be coerced into another evening in the fair Lucy's company."

"Oh, ho. So the matchmaker considers a match of his own finally?" Jared laughed heartily as he thought about Sarah's suggestion that they put those two together in order to squelch any overt matchmaking on their part.

"What's so funny?" Tom looked a little irritated at Jared's attempt at humor.

"Oh, just thought of something Sarah said a couple of weeks ago." Jared turned from the steering wheel "How about we surprise them at Pilot Oaks?"

"Do you think that's a good idea? I mean, girls usually like surprises, but only if they get advance notice, if you know what I mean." Tom sounded nervous.

"Since when are you the expert? Hey, I'm the one with the title this year, remember?" Jared noticed the serious look on Tom's face. "Hey, who's agonized over this for weeks? When did you start to worry about impressing a girl that you met yesterday?"

"Point taken. I'm with you, after all. I guess the only way I could stop you would be to arrest you, and I don't want to do the paperwork on a weekend."

"Smart man. You usually learn a lot about people when you surprise them." Jared hoped that they would be well-received.

"Yeah. Sometimes you learn good things, and sometimes you learn things you'd rather not know." Tom frowned. "You know, like what they look like without makeup on or . . . Hey! What's the deal?" Tom yelled as Jared swerved a little on the highway.

"We just met Sarah and Lucy in Sarah's car." Jared looked in the rear-view mirror to confirm his suspicions. "If I were a bettin' man, I'd lay odds that they're headed to the beach to check on the house."

"Well, so much for surprising her on Monday . . . or tonight. May as well turn around and follow them, then we can face the music tonight." Tom grinned. "No pun intended. Who knows, she may just be very appreciative of your thoughtfulness."

"I like that idea. I just hope she doesn't think it was presumptuous of me." Jared suddenly worried about her reaction. "I can always tell her it was her dad's idea." He looked at Tom for confirmation.

"Well, it kinda was, in a way." He nodded, then raised an eyebrow. "When do you plan to tell her about Annabelle?"

"I . . . haven't decided yet." Jared hesitated as he pulled his thoughts together. "Maybe surprising them tonight wasn't such a good idea, after all." As he spoke, he eased up on the accelerator.

Tom rolled his eyes. "Good grief, Jared, you can't avoid it now. Let's just go over there and reap the benefits of a thoughtful gesture, take the ladies out for dinner, and then you can show off that gorgeous beach house to Lucy. I'd imagine Sarah's told her all about it."

Jared was focused on the road and on Sarah's car that was a couple of cars ahead of them. "Let's do this, then. But listen, I'm counting on you to pray with me. I'll know when it's the right time. God's time. Sound okay?" He waited for his friend's reaction.

"Sounds good to me." Tom closed his eyes and prayed for the few minutes that it took them to get back to Sarah's little beach house at Murrells Inlet.

"THIS HOUSE IS JUST as cute as it can be, Sarah." Lucy stepped on the path to the front door. "Huh . . . look at this." She pointed to one geranium that had been crushed.

Sarah frowned. "I wonder how that happened? It wasn't like that a couple of days ago."

"A big dog, maybe? You haven't had the furniture delivered yet, so it couldn't have been them." Lucy pondered with Sarah as they looked at the poor, decimated blossom.

"Oh, well, I'll get another one next time I'm near a nursery. Come on, let's go in." Sarah began to dig in her purse for her house key. "I can't wait to show it to you!"

"I think we've got company." Lucy quirked an eyebrow as Jared's SUV pulled into the drive next to Sarah's little car. Her excitement grew when she saw that he was not alone.

Sarah looked up when she found her keys, just in time to see

Jared swing down from the vehicle. His smile made her heart almost forget to beat and her lungs forget to breathe.

He reached the porch, and before she had time to greet him, Jared reached in and kissed her gently. "Hello, beautiful," he said softly.

"I thought you were tied up today." Sarah's knees felt weak when he took her hand and drew it to his lips. His eyes never left hers.

"I got done with my . . . errand . . . earlier than I thought I would. Had a good day?" Jared touched her nose, no doubt noticing the extra freckles that had appeared on her nose because of a lazy day in the sun.

His actions had thrown her deliciously off-kilter. He'd never shown this much affection before in front of others. She decided to go along and let him take the lead. "Wonderful. I would definitely make a great beach bum." Tom and Lucy were off to the side talking quietly. It was obvious that they were determined not to interrupt this little interlude.

"Sorry we didn't call first, but we thought, if you didn't mind, we'd surprise you at Pilot Oaks, and wouldn't you know, we met you on the highway!"

"What did you have in mind?" Sarah turned to put her key in the lock to let everyone in.

"Well, we could go out, or we could go get some stuff and grill over at my place, if you'd like."

"Oh! I'd love Lucy to see your beach house, Jared. Why don't we do that?" Sarah grinned playfully. "Lucky for you two, Lucy's actually a good cook!"

"I figure with what I've got in mind, we can all get it together on the grill and enjoy the beach for a while. No real skill involved. I'll bet, Sarah, that you're probably a better cook than you make yourself out to be." Jared winked at her when she smiled happily at him.

When she opened the door, Sarah walked in and flipped on

the light switch that illuminated the living and dining area. Immediately, her eyes were drawn to the rather large piece of furniture that graced the inside wall just to their right. Her breath caught as her eyes filled with tears at this first sight of her beloved piano. It sat exactly where she had envisioned it. "Jared . . . did you do this?" She whispered her question and then looked at him in wonder.

"Well . . ." he began, but was interrupted as she flew into his arms and hugged him tightly.

"Oh Jared, how . . .?" She pulled away from his arms to lay her hands on the polished wood of the old piano. It was a rosy cherry veneer, with flowers and vines carved on the front and legs. Her fingers brushed the intricate relief on the front before opening the lid that revealed the perfect ivories.

"Actually, I can't take all the credit for this. Your dad called me and asked if I thought it would be a good idea, and told me how important it was to you. It wasn't hard to decide that we had to do it, Sarah. You've got to have your piano with you."

Jared walked over and stood behind her as she sat down on the bench and began to play bits and pieces of classics, hymns, and worship songs. When she began to play "Moonlight Sonata," he put his hands on her shoulders, and she leaned back against him, her eyes closed and a look of utter contentment on her face.

She put her hand on his, still resting on her shoulder. "Let me tell you the story of this piano and why it's so special to me."

"I'd love to hear it." Jared sat beside her, facing her as he sat opposite on the bench.

"The piano was passed to me from Granny when I was twelve years old. When Granny was a young married woman of eighteen, her young husband, my Granddaddy, had surprised her with a gift of a used, upright piano. Granny stripped the layers of varnish that blackened the outside of the cabinet. I think it is still one of the prettiest pianos I've ever seen. My uncle, years ago, replaced the ivories and tuned it well, and it is still my favorite piano to play.

"I didn't realize how much I missed my music." She was a little embarrassed by the tear that slid down her cheek, which Jared brushed away. She didn't like to cry in front of others. "And you! You and Dad! You really pulled one over on me. Was this the 'errand' you had to take care of today?"

"Yup." Jared shrugged a little. "I wasn't sure when the truck would get here, so I couldn't really make any plans."

"Are you bucking for business-partner-of-the-year or something?" Sarah narrowed her eyes a little as he stood, took her hand and pulled her up from the bench.

The gleam in his eyes unnerved her slightly. "Nope. What I'm buckin' for is a conversation for another time, Sarah Jane Crawford." He kissed her quickly, clearly delighted in the surprise he saw in her eyes, and in the slow smile that lit her face.

They had seen Lucy and Tom wander out to the back veranda and the beach. They were truly alone. Jared pulled her into his arms and kissed her tenderly.

Her day had just gone from good to amazing.

CHAPTER TWENTY-FIVE

*F*inally. Alone. On a date. They'd been out before . . . but . . .

"Lucy, does this look okay? I'm not sure." Sarah stood nervously in front of the mirror in the bedroom of her little beach house. She didn't know why she was so nervous. She'd seen Jared every day this week, and most of the week when she got back from Kentucky. But this was different. There was a different feel to the day . . . to the week . . . to the way Jared looked at her when he told her he wanted to go out with just her . . . to the leap of response she felt every time she looked at him and every time she saw him look at her.

"That looks great, but then, I liked the other three outfits you ran by me, too." Lucy laughed at the blush that covered Sarah's face. "Why are you so nervous?"

Sarah looked at herself up and down in the mirror and at Lucy's reflection as she stood behind her. "I honestly don't know. I just feel like this date is . . . different. And don't ask me in what way. I've gone out with Jared before, but this is the first time I'll have been alone with him, on a date since I got back. Do you think I've gone crazy?" Distress and nerves were making her voice shake.

"Calm down, girl! You're not crazy, just a little unbalanced." Lucy laughed again as Sarah rolled her eyes. "If it makes you feel better, I'm a little nervous about my date with Tom, too. We've never been out alone, except when we've tried really hard to leave you two alone." Lucy's eyebrows arched suggestively, making Sarah think back to last weekend, when Jared had kissed her in her living room.

"Do you think Jared . . . likes me?" She didn't want to put two and two together and get fifteen. It's not like she was desperate to find a man. She just wanted to know if he was the man.

"Does he like you?" Lucy repeated in disbelief. "Maybe you are crazy. Sarah. Honey. Do you realize that the man's face lights up when you enter a room? Do you realize that your face lights up when he enters a room? Have you seen the way he automatically holds out his hand and you go right to it?" Her voice softened. "Yeah. I think he likes you."

Sarah's emotions welled up as she thought about what Lucy said. Maybe all these things were those signs that she had looked for – ways that God told her, repeatedly, that he was "the one." She knew how her heart leapt whenever she caught a glimpse of him. She watched him take up the offering on Sunday morning, and it almost brought tears to her eyes. When he came back and sat with her afterward, he took her hand. It made her feel that if she never lived another day, she was complete. She was just so glad to be there, with him, in church. It was more than a feeling. It was the knowledge that God is good . . . all the time.

"Thanks, Luce. I needed that." She hugged Lucy and grabbed a tissue before her tears could do more damage to her carefully done makeup. "It's almost time for him to be here. I think I'll stick with this outfit. What do you think?" Sarah took a deep, cleansing breath, opening her eyes widely to get rid of unwanted puffiness.

"I think it's awesome." Lucy whispered her answer. "I think you'll knock his socks off."

Sarah gazed at her reflection. The strapless, cornflower blue sundress did things to her complexion that couldn't be duplicated and caused her hazel eyes to turn almost an azure blue in reflection. She hoped Lucy was right.

"That's the plan, Lucy. That's the plan."

JARED COULDN'T GET the smile off his face as he drove the few blocks to Sarah's house to pick her up for a long-anticipated – at least on his part – date. Tom and Lucy had double-dated with them a few times, but the two men had decided that the time had come to divide and conquer, so to speak. So Jared had decided that their best bet was to get out of town, to Charleston.

He had it all planned. They'd drive down and park at the Waterfront Park. From there he had arranged a carriage ride through the Battery, one of the most architecturally interesting parts of the oldest part of town; dine at Circa 1886, a restored carriage house on the grounds of a mansion; and a walk along the Charleston Harbor at Waterfront Park, where they would be able to relax and talk. The weather was perfect. The humidity was low for South Carolina in summer, and the sky was as clear as he'd seen it in weeks. Maybe this was one of those "signs" he had looked for.

Admittedly, he was nervous. Sarah was the first girl he'd dated in a long time; no, the first girl he'd ever dated that felt like the forever kind of girl that he had looked for all his life. Now he just had to get up the nerve to claim her as his own. How did one do that in the twenty-first century? Women these days had a mind of their own, didn't they? Was Sarah ready to settle down to a real, honest-to-goodness relationship, with him?

He thought about that first meeting. He had wanted to be angry, to shut out the woman who represented what everyone had tried to convince him was a slight on Alex's part. But then he had looked into her eyes. He saw into her soul that day, and ever since, she had drawn him gently, never realizing that she had a tender power about her that held him captive—quite willingly.

But tonight . . . He knew that tonight was going to be different. It was as if God had directed them to this point. He had built up to this ever since that first day. He prayed about it daily. He wooed her gently, and he hoped that she felt just a fraction of what he'd felt for her almost from the first time he met her on the porch at Pilot Oaks.

He chuckled as he pulled into her driveway. For the first time, he realized that the short drive gave him very little time to gather his wits about him, although proximity had its perks, too. He closed his eyes for a quick prayer that he wouldn't do anything to mess this up. His daydreams would have to wait. Now was the time to see if he couldn't put some of those dreams into action.

SARAH AND JARED were quiet as they walked, hand in hand, along the waterfront. They had had a wonderful dinner, a carriage ride through beautiful restored eighteenth- and nineteenth-century neighborhoods, and now as the sun lowered over the skyline and the park lights began to come on one by one, they were both lost in their own thoughts as contentment stole upon them. It was unexpected, but welcome.

When Sarah sighed, Jared looked at her closely. There was a

slight smile on her face, and the wind off the bay blew her hair back, away from her face. Her eyes widened when he squeezed her hand, and as she looked up at him, her smile grew.

"Penny for your thoughts?"

"Oh, good things. I'm glad to be here, tonight, with you." She turned toward him as they stopped along one of the paths in the park.

Jared caught her other hand in his. He drew both her hands up and looked at them as if he must study them carefully before he kissed her fingers on each one. "I'm glad you're here, tonight, with me, too." His left eyebrow quirked upward. He wasn't trying to hide the look of desire in his eyes. Not anymore. He grinned at the blush that he could see, even in the dim light. He took her hands and placed them gently on his chest and pulled her toward him, his eyes never leaving hers. Her eyes widened in anticipation, and he wondered at a fleeting look of fear in them that vanished as quickly as it came, only to be replaced with a look of desire that matched his own. He reached in and kissed her gently, his hands on her upper arms. Finally, he felt her hands slip up to his shoulders as she reached up to meet him halfway.

The kisses they had shared before had been the affectionate, getting-to-know-you kiss of a tentative sort – meaningful, chaste, curious. This kiss was different. This kiss begged the question of love and courtship. This kiss answered the question with a resounding "yes."

When they drew apart, they looked at one another in astonishment as they remained wrapped in one another's arms, slow smiles on both their faces. Jared stroked her cheek and brought his hand down to massage her shoulder and then her back. "You are an amazing woman, Sarah Jane Crawford." He was surprised at the emotion he felt.

"You're pretty amazing, yourself, Jared." Sarah spoke softly and then gazed at her own hand as it drifted from his shoulder to his chest. She rested it on the area of his heart and gave him a look that told him more than her words ever could. In her eyes and in her smile, he saw trust, passion, and the beginnings of love, all the things that he felt in his heart for her.

"Jared Benton?" a surly male voice said.

Into the pleasant fog of courtship came a jolt to Jared's heart that threatened to bring him to his knees. He closed his eyes for a second as he blanched, then tightened his hold on Sarah momentarily as he gave her a look of resignation that was more of a grimace.

As he turned toward the voice, Jared took Sarah's hand in his and faced the man that stood there under the light. "Hello, Rafe." Jared's voice was curt, but laced with sadness. "How are you?"

"Not as good as you, apparently. It's been a while. Glad to see you're not still pining away for Annabelle." Rafe Jernigan leered, angry sarcasm dripping from his voice. The red-haired man was a few inches shorter than Jared and a few years older.

"I assume you know this man?" Sarah raised an eyebrow, concern written across her features. The park was almost deserted, and Jared sensed her fear as she faced Rafe.

"Sarah Crawford, Rafe Jernigan. I used to date Rafe's sister, Annabelle." Jared spoke reluctantly. He was surprised to see a flash of recognition in her eyes. Through his mind came the unbidden thought, "what has she heard?" before his attention was pulled back to the angry man before them.

"Yeah. Date." Rafe's cold eyes never left Jared's face. When he finally looked away, he turned to Sarah. "This guy is a real heart-breaker, Sarah. Be careful that you don't get too close. Annabelle did, and look what happened to her."

"Jared?" Sarah looked from Rafe to Jared.

Rafe threw Jared a look that was meant to cut him down to size, and he just chuckled and shook his head when Jared stood his ground. "I'll let lover-boy tell you that whole sordid tale.

Have a nice evening, Benton." Rafe threw him another malevolent look and walked away.

When he disappeared into the darkness, Jared let out the breath he had been holding. He avoided her eyes. "I'm sorry, Sarah. That should never have happened. We should probably go now."

As he turned to walk in the direction of the parking lot, Sarah reached for his hand and tugged at it to stop him. He hadn't noticed that she hadn't moved and hadn't taken her eyes off him. "Jared . . . wait."

He turned toward her, and he looked down at the hand that held tightly to his. She stood in front of him, waiting. When he finally raised his eyes to meet her gaze, he tried, in the dim light of the street lights, to discern her thoughts. He saw fear, uncertainty, and something else that he couldn't quite identify. He prayed silently that he could tell her and that he would have the confidence to trust her with the biggest secret he'd ever kept.

RAFE JERNIGAN FRIGHTENED HER, just a little. Why did he have to show up now, of all times? Why, God? Why, when they were just beginning to explore what could be? Why, when she trusted Jared Benton more than she had any other man in her life, except her father? Why, when she craved his kiss, even after a scene such as the one they had just experienced?

She closed her eyes and shook her head as she felt tears begin to smart beneath her lashes. It irritated her. She did not want to cry right now, and she did not want this to be about her. She wanted to know, not out of curiosity – well, not entirely – but out of concern for Jared and what had obviously been a traumatic time in his life. Would Annabelle come back? Did she have a prior claim? Would she potentially keep her from knowing what it would be like to be loved by this man?

Her eyes still closed, she felt Jared's hand on her cheek. His thumb stroked it as if to comfort her. His voice was rough with emotion. "I'm sorry, Sarah. If I could start the evening over and avoid that, I would."

CHAPTER TWENTY-SIX

*S*arah's eyes flew opened at his words, and she saw the sadness etched into his face. "Would you avoid everything?" She couldn't keep the impatience out of her voice, but she was gladdened by the look of surprise and confusion that crossed his face.

"No, I wouldn't avoid everything." He welcomed her back into his arms, holding her tightly as if he were afraid she would disappear. "I definitely wouldn't avoid everything. I'm just sorry that you had to be burdened with this."

She pulled back to look up at him. "You don't have to tell me what he was talking about. I respect that you have lived thirty years before you knew me. I know you didn't crawl out from under a rock the day I arrived on the scene, so it stands to reason that you would have had some . . . relationships---"

"Sarah," Jared interrupted before she could continue. "I know what you're doing. You're trying to respect my privacy."

"I trust you, Jared." She put her hand to his cheek to emphasize her point.

"Well, maybe you shouldn't. I really didn't want to tell you all this right now. I wish it would just go away, but it's not going to.

There will always be reminders. If I don't tell you . . . well, what will what we have be based on?" He took a deep breath.

"Sarah, Annabelle was my girlfriend while I was in college. She was a couple of years younger than me, and we started dating the summer I graduated from high school, and I was so busy at school with football and my job, that I never really broke up with her. Are you sure you want to hear old history?"

"Where is Annabelle now?" Sarah dreaded to hear what she was afraid was true, after having seen Rafe's attitude toward Jared.

"She's dead, Sarah."

Sarah's eyes widened with shock. "I'm sorry, Jared. What happened? I mean, apparently there was something, if the encounter with Rafe is any indication." She wanted to soothe him, wanted it to go away, but part of her needed to know for her own peace of mind. Annabelle was dead. She wouldn't come back, so why was this still an emotional issue for Jared and Rafe? Was the love Jared had for her so strong that he felt he couldn't love again?

Jared caressed Sarah's cheek as if to comfort both of them. "Car accident. But that's not what Rafe's still angry about. Sarah, it was ten years ago." He looked away for a second, a glint of tears in his eyes. "Annabelle was eighteen, I was twenty. Rafe doesn't know the whole story."

"But---"

He shook his head and snorted. "Even I didn't know until it was too late. She was sleeping with a guy she graduated with. You want to know the real kicker? When I found out she had cheated on me, I didn't really feel anything. Everybody assumed that once I got out of school and went to law school, we'd get married and live happily ever after. I guess when I was eighteen and she was sixteen, it sounded like a great idea. By the time we'd had a couple of years of a long-distance relationship, we just kind of drifted, you know?"

"Were you in love with her?"

"No. I know that, now. We drifted into a relationship, and then drifted right out of it. We'd never had a . . . physical . . . relationship, so I have no regrets, there. We came close a few times, but I really thought she was committed to wait for marriage for that part of the equation." Jared paused, but when she squeezed his hand, he continued.

Jared nodded when he saw the resolve in her eyes and the hint of gladness at his revelation. "I went to pick her up for a date not long after I got back into town from school, and when I got to her house, I saw her black eye. Her parents were out of town, so she was at home alone. She tried to cover it up with makeup, but when you play football and see as many bruises as I have, you recognize other signs. She tried to stay turned to one side. Thought I wouldn't notice. When I asked her about it, she cried. I had noticed that she had been . . . different . . . when I talked to her on the phone, but thought it was just the whole graduation thing. She'd just turned eighteen, you know. I half-expected it when she told me she wanted to break up with me. What I didn't expect was for her to break down when I pressed her about the eye."

A bleak look came back into his face as he led Sarah over to a park bench. Sarah rubbed his back and tried to comfort him with her touch. He raised his head as he sat with his elbows planted on his knees, fingers laced together between them.

"She knew she could count on you, didn't she?" He nodded, but put his head back down. She could tell that he didn't want to face her right now. "Jared, what happened after that?"

Tears were on his lashes as he looked away into the distance. He was making a decision, she knew. Was it too much?

Jared plunged in. "She told me that she was pregnant, and that she'd gotten the black eye when she told the baby's father about the baby. He wanted her to get rid of it. Annabelle hadn't done everything perfectly, but she didn't believe in abortion.

217

This was her baby . . . part of her. She wanted to take responsibility for what she'd done – for what they had done. She didn't want to tell me. She planned to go away quietly, after she broke up with me, leave town, and start a new life." Jared spoke as if the words had been ripped from him. "I told her she didn't have to do that, that I'd marry her, and we'd raise the baby together. She didn't want to make me look bad. As if I cared, at that point."

"How did the accident happen?" Sarah prompted him to continue as he stopped and stared straight ahead, lost in his thoughts. She was surprised when he reached over and took her hand. He pulled it into both of his as he stared at it, gently stroked it, and traced her knuckles and fingers absently as he remained hunched over on the bench.

"I offered to take her to some friends' house in Charleston. She couldn't get up the nerve to tell her parents about the baby and didn't want them to see her with a black eye. She thought if she could just have some breathing space for a week or so, make some decisions about the future, then she could come back and face the music. She didn't need the pressure of her parents and everyone in town that thought they knew what the best thing was for her. It rained that night. We were on our way to Charleston when the accident happened. Remember that straight, flat stretch before you get to the outskirts of Charleston? It happened not too far from Boone Plantation, where there's little but trees on either side of the road. I hit some standing water on the road, hydroplaned, ran off the road and hit a tree. No airbags. It knocked us both out, and it was a while before anybody saw the car and called an ambulance." Jared had grown calm in the telling.

"I don't remember anything about the crash after my head hit the windshield. I woke up in the ambulance. I asked about Annabelle, and they told me she was in the other ambulance – the one that came first."

Sarah could see the horror in his eyes at the memory. "Sarah, I found out later they had to cut her out of the car. When we got to the hospital, they checked me out and just kept me overnight for observation. Concussion was all I had. I couldn't get anybody to tell me about Annabelle. The next morning, when I woke up, Mom and Dad were there. They had been in DC. Dad had a meeting at the Pentagon, and they drove all night from DC to get there. They told me that she was in a coma, and that she might be brain-dead. I think that was the worst day of my life."

"I can't even imagine how you felt." Sarah didn't realize that tears had escaped her lashes until she felt his fingers wiping them away. This man who sat beside her had gone through this horror when he was little more than a boy. No wonder he was so careful when it came to relationships.

"They released me from the hospital, and I went down to ICU to see Annabelle. Her parents and Rafe were there. They didn't notice her black eye, because she was bruised almost beyond recognition anyway. They had found out she was pregnant and assumed it was mine. I didn't tell them any different. I thought she would somehow wake up and straighten it all out, and then I thought I didn't want them to have to know what she'd done. As angry as they were with me, I thought maybe I could shield her from some of the anger they would have for her for getting pregnant. And not only that, but the baby wasn't even mine. It wasn't the child of her boyfriend, but a boy who would not only get her pregnant, but also abuse her. I couldn't trade my reputation for hers. Not then, and I guess, not ever." He shrugged. "My only regret is that anyone who shares my name will share that reputation . . . that dirty little secret . . . that everyone thinks is true."

"But Jared, your intentions were the best." Sarah sat there and tried to wrap her head around his story.

"Yeah, well, you know what they say. The road to Hell is

paved with good intentions." His voice was bitter for the first time in the telling. "Annabelle died about a week later. She had already lost the baby. They finally established that there was no brain activity, and they pulled the plug. It didn't take long. After she died, I didn't want to sully their memories of her any more than it already was by telling them what she'd done. I was young, I wasn't thinking straight, and the few people who knew the facts thought I was crazy, but I stuck to my guns. I don't know, maybe they were right." He shrugged wearily. "To me, it was the next right thing."

"Sometimes the next right thing is the only thing you can do." Sarah squeezed his hand and laid her cheek on his shoulder.

"Anyway, after that, her parents moved to Beaufort, and Rafe lives around here somewhere. I've seen them from time to time. Her parents wouldn't speak to me at the time and still avoid contact, and Rafe still carries a lot of resentment. He blames me for her death."

"That's crazy. I mean . . ." Sarah huffed at him, finally getting a ghost of a smile from him.

"Yeah, well. Honestly, there have been times that I wish it had been me, instead of Annabelle, but it wasn't. There have been times that I've wanted to tell them the truth, but then I think 'what's the use?' It wouldn't make me feel any better and would only hurt them. Alex wanted me to tell them, but I couldn't. When he finally resigned himself that I wouldn't do it, he accepted it and told me that God wasn't finished with me yet. I think that helped me through that time more than anything." He gazed down at their linked hands.

"I miss him, and I never even met him." Sarah sighed wistfully. "Sometimes I could use some of that wisdom myself."

Jared gave her a questioning look. She put her hand on his cheek, and he pulled her into his arms and hugged her tightly. She snuggled her face into the crook of his neck as she sought to comfort him. He stroked her cheek as he wiped away the tears she had shed on his behalf. He bent to kiss her lips tenderly, but with a new intensity. "Thank you, Sarah."

"For what, Jared?" Sarah knew that she wouldn't have been anywhere else at this moment.

"For being here. I didn't want to, but I needed to tell you now, before you heard parts of it from someone else. Thank you for your tears. You're a special lady, you know." He looked down at the hand that had made its way back to his chest. When he looked back at her, she could still see fear there. "I have to ask you something, though."

"What's that?" She wanted so badly to rub away all the pain and fear in his eyes. Would he let her do that for him?

"Will it make a difference?" He looked deeply into her eyes.

"A difference in what?" Confusion settled in.

"In how you look at me. In how you feel about me. Will it bother you, what other people think is true?" He narrowed his eyes as if to ward off more hurt.

Sarah reached over and cupped his cheek with her hand and kissed his lips tenderly, carefully, then smiled at him a little sadly. She couldn't help but worry that this would eventually eat him up inside. It would probably resurface from time to time, but she knew instinctively what he needed to hear from her. It was as if God had whispered the words into her ear.

"Yeah, it makes a difference, but not the way you think. I'm tougher than that, Jared. I guess in the grand scheme of things I haven't known you that long, and I may not have had much experience in matters of the heart, but I know a good man when I see one. The man I know is not the twenty-year-old with a traumatic experience in his past, but the thirty-year-old who serves in his church and in his community, who helps elderly ladies find worth in their lives, who makes strangers feel a part of a community . . ." She paused, a flirty glint in her eye as she tried to cheer him just a bit. ". . . and who, by the way, is an excellent grill-master as well as kisser."

Her list was interrupted by a kiss from Jared that told her just how much it mattered to him that she could see beyond the story that he had harbored for so long. That her opinion mattered to him told her more than she dared hope so early in their relationship. It told her that this, indeed, a relationship to cherish.

CHAPTER TWENTY-SEVEN

"*S*o . . . how was the date?"

It had been the wee hours of the morning before Sarah and Jared had made their way back to Sarah's house. When they returned from Charleston, they drove to Pilot Oaks and took a walk on the private beach there, then sat in the summerhouse and talked a while. They never quite broke physical contact.

Sarah thought about it as she tried to settle down to sleep. She realized that what he had shared with her, this most horrific chapter of his life, was almost a test. He wasn't testing her. Himself, maybe? God? Whatever it was, Jared couldn't quite end the evening, and Sarah didn't want to, either. A bond that started to grow on the front porch of Pilot Oaks had taken a turn this evening, and somehow, they both knew that their relationship would never be the same after this.

"It was . . . good." She wasn't ready to share with Lucy what they had experienced. Some of it she would never share, but she could let her know that she was happy. She looked at her friend with a brilliant smile and said with confidence, "It was really good. What about your date?"

"I had a great time." Lucy scrunched her face in confusion and then turned a serious look on Sarah. "How do you know if you've found 'the one?'?"

Sarah was a little taken aback at the question. "Are you talking about me or you?"

"Hypothetically speaking—unless there's something you'd like to share?" Lucy arched an eyebrow at her best friend.

Sarah decided to latch on to the hypothetical aspect of the question. "Hmmm . . . well, considering I have even less dating experience than you, that's a tough one. I . . . I guess you just . . . know? What do you think?" Sarah frowned a bit in slight consternation.

"You're probably right." Lucy flounced onto the blue leather sofa and wailed in despair. "Oh, Sarah, I don't want to go home!"

"Is that the depressed-vacationer-seeing-the-trip-home-looming talking or the girl-who-thinks-she-may-have-found-'the one' talking?" Sarah laughed in surprise at the expression on Lucy's face, which was a mixture of hope, depression, fear, and anticipation.

"You know, I think it's a little bit of both. I did have a great time with Tom." Lucy covered her face for a second before looking up at her. "Um . . . he kissed me, Sarah." Lucy blushed, and then held up her hands when she saw Sarah's eyebrows shoot up. "It was just a quick kiss, but it was wonderful."

"Wow! I mean . . . Wow! So then what happened?" Sarah perched on the arm of the sofa and took on the role usually commandeered by Lucy in the matchmaking department.

"We walked along the boardwalk at Myrtle Beach, and he held my hand. He was such a perfect gentleman, Sarah. I could have just melted into a puddle and been swept out to sea, I was so content." Lucy sighed happily, until a dark cloud seemed to settle over her face. "And then it came to me that I've already signed my letter of intent to return to school this fall, so it's the end. Life's a bummer, isn't it?"

"Sometimes." Sarah nodded and then looked out the window at the waves as they crashed on the beach and the seagulls as they flew, deep in thought as she considered what to say, and whether she had a right to say anything. If last night had taught her anything, it was that life's too short not to be there for a friend when needed. With a slight frown and a bit of uncertainty, she decided to forge ahead. "You know, Luce, if Tom's the guy God has for you, a little more time won't hurt anything."

"Yeah, says the girl who has her cake and is eating it, too." Lucy rolled her eyes in irritation when she saw the half-smile on Sarah's face. "You're not the one that has to leave tomorrow. You get to see Jared every day. It's just not fair. I'm thrilled for you, but aggravated at the same time."

"Sorry, Luce. You know it's not always been that way. Maybe if you focus on my past stellar failures, it'll make you feel better," Sarah teased and finally saw a reluctant grin break through on Lucy's face.

"So, I've told you about my date. What about yours? You have a rather contented, dreamy look on your face this morning, too, and I don't think it's because of the stellar Sunday school lesson we have to be there for in . . . oh . . . an hour and a half?" Lucy drummed her fingers on the arm of the couch and looked at Sarah expectantly.

Sarah checked her watch and realized that they would, indeed, have to kick up the pace if they were to make it for Bible study this morning. "Like I said earlier, it was really good, Luce." Her mind traveled back, and she blushed at the memory of Jared's kisses the night before.

"Yeah, and if that faraway look in your eyes means anything, then last night was more than 'good,' and that you may have just found 'the one' for you." Lucy turned on her heel and yelled over her shoulder, "Dibs on the shower!"

WHEN SARAH and Lucy arrived in the church parking lot with about two minutes to spare, Sarah's face lit up when she saw Jared's car right behind them. A smile graced her lips as he swung up out of the car and make his way to her.

"Good morning." Jared said as he reached for her hand to help her out of the car. "Looks like we're both late for Sunday school!"

"That's what happens when you keep a girl out too late." Lucy laughed.

"I'm as much to blame as Jared," Sarah admitted, her cheeks warming.

"True, but I did kind of shanghai you when we got back to town last night. It was just too nice a night not to go for a walk on the beach, didn't you think?" He held a hand out to her as they made their way to the front door.

"Definitely." Sarah automatically took his hand and gave it a squeeze. It was so natural. It was as if they'd been together forever, and right now, if anyone had asked her where they were headed, she would have simply answered, "anywhere with Jared."

"Go to lunch after service?" Jared asked.

"How about you and Tom come over and we'll cook something up?" Sarah raised her eyebrows as she glanced over at Lucy.

"Sounds good. How about I bring some steaks over to grill?"

"Sounds like my favorite grill-master is ready to be put to work." Sarah smiled and wiggled her eyebrows slightly as he laughed.

Jared squeezed her hand again before he let it go to open the door for the two ladies. As Sarah passed in front of him, he put his hand on the small of her back, leaned toward her, and whispered in her ear, "and if we play our cards right, we might just get to try out some of those other talents that you seem to think I have." She shivered slightly at his touch.

"I'm pretty good at cards." Sarah said it quietly, and a soft giggle gurgled up through her lips. "Now behave."

"Yes, ma'am." He gave her a jaunty salute before they entered the classroom full of single adults. Now if he could just get his mind back on the matters at hand – today's lesson. Wouldn't you know it would be on patience . . .?

CHAPTER TWENTY-EIGHT

*S*arah drove back from Charleston on Monday with a song on her lips as she bopped along to the local Christian radio station. She had taken Lucy to the airport that morning. They had said a tearful goodbye, but each girl knew that it wouldn't be long before they saw one another again. The tears were almost happy, excited tears—tears that spoke of obstacles overcome.

She knew Lucy had worried a little about leaving her behind to go home. But she also knew that after the weekend, and really ever since they had returned to Murrells Inlet with her earthly possessions, that Lucy would be able to reassure her family back home that she was, indeed, where God had planted her. Life was good.

"Okay, God, it's you and me here for a little while, and I've got a few things to discuss with You, if You don't mind." She turned off the radio and prayed out loud. She had about a half-hour drive ahead of her, and she was out of city traffic and on the straight, flat road that ran almost parallel to the coast between Charleston and Georgetown, South Carolina.

She was struck with the notion to pray when she saw the

signs for Boone Plantation and reached that stretch of road that Jared had told her about. The area where the accident happened that had changed his outlook on life and affected hers as well, after the unplanned meeting with Annabelle's brother.

"I know You love me, and I know You love Jared. We have evidence of that all around us. I know You want the best for us. Lord . . . is Jared that 'best' that you have for me? Honestly, I can't imagine him not being the best . . . I think I love him, Lord . . . and I think he may love me, too, just a little bit . . ."

"I think he loves you more than 'just a little bit,' Sarah."

"Okay, maybe. What can I do to help him know that what other people whisper about him doesn't affect me? I see who he is now. I see the man who has faced fear and misunderstanding and has come out a thoughtful, mature, loving man."

"He will understand that, Sarah. He knows that you see beyond what the gossips say about him, about his relationship with Annabelle. That's part, but not all, of what he loves about you. Let him know you have confidence in him. Let him know that you trust him."

"I do, Father. I do trust him, and I would trust him with my life."

Sarah felt the tears begin to fall down her cheeks as she realized that, for her, any fear she had of a commitment to someone for life had been obliterated in the face of the fear and remorse Jared had let her see in his own life on that fateful Saturday night.

Although Sarah had never been considered a selfish individual and had usually put the good of others before herself, she realized, for the first time, that she had finally found someone that mattered even more to her than she meant to herself. She hadn't had those thoughts of discontentment, of longing for something "more," since she'd come back from Kentucky that last time.

Actually, it was before that. As she looked back, it was really since Jared called her on the phone that morning while he ran on the beach. After that, all she wanted was to get back here, to South Carolina, to him. "Thank You, Lord. Thank You. I love You, Lord, and I don't know what else to do right now except praise You."

"Is JARED IN HIS OFFICE?" Sarah asked as she entered Crawford and Benton. Carla looked a bit startled when she saw Sarah's tear-stained face.

"Yes, he just got back in a few minutes ago. I think he was on the phone, but he's off now." She glanced down at the phone to check for blinking lights. "You okay?"

"I'm fine . . . really. It's been an emotional day, and I took Lucy to the airport this morning. Thanks, Carla." She fluttered her hand at her as she made her way back to the suite of offices that she and Jared shared.

When she was almost there, she stopped in the hallway. She was thankful that she had avoided anyone as she put her hand over her heart only to feel the almost frantic beat that threatened to take her breath away. She took a deep breath and wiped the tears from her eyes, then walked into the office and closed the door behind her. Jared looked up at her with a ready smile, but it faded when he saw her face. He looked worried as he stood up immediately and went to her.

"You've been crying." He spoke bluntly as he walked toward her. When he reached out and took her hand in his, he wiped tears from her face with his other hand. "Are you okay?"

She beamed as she reached in to kiss him on the lips. This was where she would begin the process of reassurance to this man that she loved him, and that she was, indeed, better than okay. "Jared, you may as well get used to tears on this face. I cry when I'm sad, I cry when I'm happy, I cry when I'm frustrated, and I cry when I've talked to God . . . which I've done all the way back from Charleston. Those are the tears that mean not only have I talked to Him, but that I've listened, too."

He groaned as he pulled her into a tight hug. "Oh, Sarah, I was afraid . . ."

"Afraid of what? I thought fear was my department?" Sarah pulled back to search his face.

He looked down for a minute. "I was afraid once Lucy left."

"You were afraid I'd regret the move . . . that I'd decide to go back home . . . and that I'd leave . . ." Sarah spoke softly from the circle of his arms.

"That you'd leave me." Jared nodded slightly as he clutched her even more tightly. "I don't know if I could stand that."

"I don't know if I could, either." She spoke in a whisper and cupped his cheek with her hand as she felt tears begin to fall once again. "There are those tear ducts again. I'm not sad, I'm not frustrated, and I'm not praying . . . wonder what kind of tears they are?"

"I hope they're happy tears. Happy that you're here, with me?" He was hesitant.

"I think you're right. I am happy, here, with you, Jared."

"I love you, Sarah."

The tears that had begun as a gentle trickle began to fall in earnest as Sarah's smile grew wider at Jared's unexpected admission. She had patiently waited for the man God had for her. She expected a timetable of courtship and eventually, admissions of love. And now, here was this man that she had dreamed of such a short time ago. And he had told her that he loved her.

Delight yourself in the Lord, and He will give you the desires of your heart.

God had given her the desire to find a man worthy to be called "husband." He had given her the desire for a man who would care for her and who could depend on her for

232

reassurance and encouragement. He had given her the desire, in the form of a dream, for this particular man, in this particular place. He had reassured her, again, even today, that this was the man He had saved for her, out of all the men in the world. Sarah knew, as she had never known or experienced before, that God loved his children as a group, but even more, He loved his children as individuals. She knew, today, that He loved her and wanted the best for her. Jared *was* the best, and he had just told her that he loved her.

"Sarah?" Jared's eyes still held that look of fear that he had become so adept at hiding.

"Jared, I love you, too." She smiled at him and felt his tensed muscles relax under her touch.

"I was afraid I had moved too fast."

Sarah shook her head. "No, not too fast at all. In fact, your timing was perfect. I didn't tell you what I prayed about, did I?"

He looked down at her, the relief in his tone and on his face evidence of the shift from abject fear to utter relief. "No, you didn't. Anything I'd be interested in?"

"I think so. Do you remember that verse from Psalm 37? 'Delight yourself in the Lord, and He will give you the desires of your heart?'"

"Sure. It's always been one of my favorites. It took me a long time to realize that it didn't mean what I thought it did at first." Jared shrugged, but still watched her closely.

"You mean what I used to think – that if you were good, and did all the right things, that God would give you what you wanted? I thought that, too. I realize, now, that it really means that He gives us *His* desires – not the 'stuff' we think we desire. Does that make sense?" She felt like she wasn't putting it well. She frowned as she tried to figure out how to put into words what had been going through her mind the last few days.

"That's the way I've learned to interpret it. Not quite the same thing that we thought as teenagers, huh?" He laughed and pulled her closer and placed a gentle kiss on her nose as she smiled up at him.

She wasn't sure just how to put this, but she knew that to assure him that she trusted him with all that was within her, she had to come clean and be completely honest with him. "Jared, I realized something today in my little prayer meeting with God on the highway. I realized just what that desire in my heart has been and is. It's . . . you."

She watched the light in his eyes grow, and she knew that she had done what she was supposed to do. *"Thank you, God."* She prayed silently. *"Thank you for guiding me. Thank you for giving me the desire of my heart."*

"Sarah Jane Crawford." He had to stop to clear his throat as emotion roughened his voice. "It may be too soon to tell you this, but I have to. I love you more than I've ever loved another human being. I know it was no accident that we saw one another for the first time on the beach instead of Pilot Oaks. It was no accident that your Uncle Alex, whom you never had the good fortune to meet, took me under his wing and helped me get started in business and in just about every other way. It was no accident that you met Rainey Thompson and she invited you to church. It was no accident that we met up with Rafe Jernigan the other night. If not for that, we'd probably still be dabbling in the shallows, me afraid to tell you of what it was I was so afraid. God has pulled us together all our lives, and we've just now caught up with Him."

Sarah gave him a glorious smile and simply said, "Amen."

Jared bent his head to hers and caught her lips in a caress that left them both breathless. They knew, somehow, that the love that had been fanned into flame between them was a love that they had never experienced before and that they wouldn't have with anyone else. This was a love to last a lifetime.

"Jared." Sarah had a glint in her eye as she realized that they had, somehow, moved from an upright position in the middle of the office to a seated position, close together on the leather sofa that graced his office.

"Yes, sweetheart."

"I never told you this, but I saw you once, before we actually met on the beach, and then at the house."

"You mean before Oliver nearly ran me down on the boardwalk?" Jared's happiness was infectious.

"Nope. It was even earlier." She drew him even closer, if that were possible.

"Oh, really?" Curiosity was written all over his face. "And when was this?" He took every opportunity to kiss her as he held her, still, in the circle of his arms.

As she reached over to once again stroke his cheek with her hand, Sarah gazed at him before she kissed him first sweetly and tenderly, and then more passionately before she said to him, "I saw you in my dreams, darling . . . in my dreams."

THE END -

ABOUT THE AUTHOR

Regina Merrick began reading romance and thinking of book
ideas as early as her teenage years when she attempted a
happily-ever-after sequel to "Gone With the Wind." That love of
fiction parlayed into a career as both a school and public
librarian, and more recently, as a full-time author. Married for
nearly 35 years and active in their local church, Regina and her
retired-teacher husband have two grown daughters who share
her love of music, writing, and the arts. She resides in a 100-
year-old house in Marion, KY with her husband and their dog,
Cedric, whose late litter-mate, Oliver, was the model for Sarah's
Schnauzer-mix.

Carolina Mercy

A Southern Breeze Series—Book Two

She's always gotten everything she's wanted. He thinks he has to give up everything. Her best friend's wedding is foremost on Lucy Dixon's radar. Her biggest concern is once again meeting Tom Livingston, who has ignored her since an idyllic date on the boardwalk of Myrtle Beach the previous summer. At least, it is her biggest concern until tragedy strikes. Where is her loving, merciful God, now?

When Tom Livingston meets Lucy, the attraction is instant. Soon after, his mother is diagnosed with an untreatable illness, and his personal life is pushed aside. His work with the sheriff's department, his family—they are more important. He knows about the love of God, but circumstances make him feel as if God's mercy is for everyone else, not him. Can a wedding and a hurricane—blessing and tragedy—bring them together?

Carolina Grace

A Southern Breeze Series—Book Three

First-year Special Education teacher Charly Livingston demonstrates God's love on the outside but is resentful that God allowed back-to-back tragedies in her family.

Rance Butler is a top-notch medical intern. He's on his way to the top, and when he meets Charly, he knows things will only get better. When he discovers family secrets and a dying father he never knew, his easy, carefree life seems to disintegrate.

Even in the idyllic ocean breezes and South Carolina sunshine, contentment turns to bitterness and confusion except for God's amazing grace.

Scrivenings
PRESS
Quench your thirst for story.
www.ScriveningsPress.com

Stay up-to-date on your favorite books and authors with our free e-newsletters.

ScriveningsPress.com

Made in the USA
Monee, IL
22 June 2023

36310655R00138